Destination
New York City

Destination New York City

A Destination Murder Mystery

Ann Shepphird

4 Horsemen
Publications, Inc.

Destination New York City
Destination Murder Mysteries Book 4
Copyright © 2025 Ann Shepphird. All rights reserved.

4 Horsemen
Publications, Inc.

Published By: 4 Horsemen Publications, Inc.

4 Horsemen Publications, Inc.
PO Box 417
Sylva, NC 28779
4horsemenpublications.com
info@4horsemenpublications.com

Cover & Typesetting by Autumn Skye
Edited by Jen Paquette

All rights to the work within are reserved to the author and publisher. No part of this publication may be reproduced, stored in a retrieval system, or transmitted in any form or by any means, electronic, mechanical, photocopying, recording, scanning, or otherwise, except as permitted under Section 107 or 108 of the 1976 International Copyright Act, without prior written permission except in brief quotations embodied in critical articles and reviews. Please contact either the Publisher or Author to gain permission.

All characters, organizations, and events portrayed in this novel are either products of the author's imagination or are used fictitiously. No generative artificial intelligence was used in the creation of this book or its cover.

All brands, quotes, and cited work respectfully belongs to the original rights holders and bear no affiliation to the authors or publisher.

Library of Congress Control Number: 2025945335

Paperback ISBN-13: 979-8-8232-0991-5
Hardcover ISBN-13: 979-8-8232-0992-2
Ebook ISBN-13: 979-8-8232-0993-9

For the most amazing New Yorkers I know, Frances Hill Barlow and Martha Ann Babcock

Mixing travel elements into a mystery novel comes with its challenges. I want to provide as full and accurate a description of each destination as possible while also telling a good story that (by necessity) includes a little murder and mayhem. For this reason, in "Destination New York City"—and all the books in the Destination Murder Mystery series—I've attempted to combine the two by creating a fictional world within the larger destination. In this case, while evocative of the amazing historic hotels in New York City, The Françoise and all the action that takes place there is a total product of my imagination.

My thanks, as always, to all who helped bring this book to life, especially Jill Bastian and Sally Braley, whose feedback on early drafts improved the book immeasurably. Thanks also to my editor, Jen Paquette, and to Laura Mita, Erika Lance, Jason Gewirtz, Jane Wortman, Jordan Weiner, and Jeff Wolf.

TABLE OF CONTENTS

CHAPTER ONE 1
CHAPTER TWO 16
CHAPTER THREE 24
CHAPTER FOUR 39
CHAPTER FIVE 54
CHAPTER SIX 68
CHAPTER SEVEN 81
CHAPTER EIGHT 93
CHAPTER NINE 103
CHAPTER TEN 111
CHAPTER ELEVEN 123
CHAPTER TWELVE 135
CHAPTER THIRTEEN 145
CHAPTER FOURTEEN 159
CHAPTER FIFTEEN 171
CHAPTER SIXTEEN 181
CHAPTER SEVENTEEN 194
CHAPTER EIGHTEEN 207

CHAPTER NINETEEN................217
CHAPTER TWENTY..................226

BOOK CLUB QUESTIONS............233
ABOUT THE AUTHOR 235

CHAPTER ONE

The noise. That's the first thing I noticed. It had been a while since I had been to New York City, and as I came out of the train station in Midtown Manhattan, I was met with a cacophony of sounds that stopped me in my tracks. From the cars and their horns and the construction workers and their jackhammers to the hordes of people speaking loudly in a variety of languages amid the sirens in the distance, it was a total assault on the auditory senses. Especially if you compared it to Carmel-by-the-Sea, California, where the most prevalent sound was the lapping of the waves outside our family home near Carmel Point.

No lapping waves in New York. Well, there are lapping waves—it's surrounded by water, for god's sake—but you sure don't hear them over the symphony of concrete and metal and humankind. Unless, of course, you find yourself locked in a small sealed room below street level. There, as I learned the hard way, you will find absolute silence. That silence might have been enjoyable except for the fact that I was trapped down there with no food or water or phone connection in a locked room not scheduled to be opened for at least a week. Even worse, no one knew I was there—except, of course, the person who locked me in there, who I had recently discovered was a murderer. Yep, you heard me. Murderer.

As I calculated the number of days I could live without water (in case you're wondering, it's three) and wishing I had taken a few more sips of the stuff when I'd had the chance, I went over the series of events that led me—Samantha "Sam" Powers—into this predicament.

My trip to New York began, as most of my trips do, with a request from my editor at *Carmel Today* magazine, Mona Reynolds. It wasn't a typical assignment. As the magazine's part-time travel columnist, I was usually asked to write about a hotel or a destination based on an invitation to cover it via a press trip (also called a "fam" or familiarization trip) or individual visit. Even the local Monterey Peninsula hotels and restaurants and attractions I wrote about for the front-of-book "Out and About" section of the magazine tended to come via press releases touting an opening or renovation—the common theme being they included something newsy to share with our readers. No, this one was different.

Chapter One

To begin with, I wasn't originally supposed to be in New York at all. This was Mona's trip. As the editor-in-chief of a luxury lifestyle magazine, *Carmel Today*'s market niche, she had been asked to speak at a fancy schmancy conference being held at a fancy schmancy hotel overlooking Central Park. The conference was one that a friend of Mona's had created and run for decades called the Business of Luxury. As the name suggests, it brought together the various entities catering to the luxury lifestyle market to mingle and discuss the latest trends in the industry for both the buyers (retailers, corporate gift curators, travel agents, meeting planners) and sellers (hotels and resorts, fashion and design entities, and other purveyors of stuff the luxury set likes, such as fine wine and cuisine).

Mona spoke at the conference often. After thirty years as a features editor at *Vogue* magazine and five as the editor-in-chief for *Carmel Today*, she knew how to spot industry trends with the best of them. Plus, this year the conference was being held at The Françoise, a historic hotel built more than a hundred years ago and recently purchased and renovated by a luxury hotel chain based in Europe. Since the hotel had just reopened following an extensive restoration, it made sense that Mona would cover it—and New York City—for the "Splendid Adventures" feature I usually wrote for the magazine. Two birds, one stone, as they say.

So, yeah, Mona took the trip. And I was fine with it. Really, I was. Not only was it a good excuse for her to visit all the friends she made during her time living in the city, but tall, elegant, and oh-so-fashionable Mona was also a much more appropriate speaker for a conference called the Business of Luxury than I ever would have been. That and she still enjoyed penning the occasional story and knew which aspects of the city to highlight for the readers in the magazine. All good.

Of course, that left me back in good ole Carmel-by-the-Sea, adorable hamlet that it is. With our spring issue off to the printer, I found myself in the office helping the competing personalities in the editorial and art departments with a final proofread. Mona had already signed off on all the stories, so each of us took a last pass through the pages to make sure nothing egregiously awful snuck through during the production process. I took a close look at the headers and footers, headlines and captions, knowing that sometimes editors spend so much time poring over a possible missed comma in the body copy that their eyes gloss over a glaring typo sitting there in 48-point type in a headline or (even worse) on the cover. It happened more often than we would have liked back at the Los Angeles newspaper where I worked as an investigative reporter for ten years before returning home to Carmel. And, let me tell you, readers love pointing out those mistakes.

The issue looked good. It included the scintillating (if I do say so myself) "Splendid Adventures" feature that came out of my recent trip to the Lake Tahoe Mountain Lodge as well as some smaller stories I'd written for the "Out and About" section. After taking an eagle eye to my own stories, I read through the rest

Chapter One

of the magazine. I found a few errant extra spaces and thought about our former managing editor, Tom—a.k.a. Toupee Tom (yes, I had nicknames for everyone on staff)—and how he'd be proud of me. He would be even more proud to learn that I then circumvented our annoying assistant-editor-slash-niece-of-the-owners Chelsea (Fuck You Chelsea a.k.a. FU Chelsea) and went straight to our new and very competent managing editor Katie (Captain Katie) to let her know.

Once Katie pushed the button that would send all our InDesign files to the printer, the staff gathered for a "happy dance of completion" (my contribution—not sure how the others felt about it) and a quick toast with some local sparkling wine. "Don't call it champagne if it's not from the Champagne region in France!" FU Chelsea said, literally every time we drank it. I think you can see how she got her moniker. Not a group typically prone to a lot of hanging out together, we headed off on our separate ways.

As I was leaving, Katie told me that I could have the rest of the week off. The truth is, there was nothing for me to do until Mona returned and we had our editorial meeting to go over the assignments for the next issue anyway. With Mona covering the New York hotel, I didn't even have a feature story to research and write, so I started home feeling a little out of sorts.

I didn't go straight home. First, I stopped by my friend Lizzy's dog-friendly café, the Paws Up, located in downtown Carmel a few blocks from the magazine's office. Fortunately for her (but not for me), the place was super busy. There seemed to be some kind of local "pug crawl"—yes, pugs as in the dogs—gathering at her place before making its way to the other dog-friendly establishments in town. I wasn't in the mood to fight a bunch of bodies (human and canine) just to chat with Lizzy, so I gave her a quick wave and motioned that I was heading back out.

Fine. Next, I walked down Carmel-by-the-Sea's main drag, Ocean Avenue. Filled with cute shops, restaurants, wine tasting rooms, and art galleries, it could be sleepy or bustling depending on how many tourists were in town. A tourist bus had obviously recently let out as the sidewalks were crowded with lookie-loos, including those who thought it a good idea to stop abruptly to take a picture.

Yes, it's a very cute storybook cottage with a candy store inside—now could we move it along? I thought. Between the pugs and the people, Carmel was bustling, and I was most definitely not in a bustling mood. I did say hello to the dogs I came into contact with. I am not a complete monster.

I turned on the side street that led to my dad's assisted living facility. As I entered the doors into the locked memory care section, I found the common area empty and the head nurse, Alejandra, by herself in the nurse's station.

"Hey Alejandra."

"Hey Sam."

"Quiet in here."

"Blissful, huh?"

"Where is everybody?"

"Most are in the van taking a drive through Pebble Beach."

Chapter One

"And my dad?" I asked, bracing myself for the response. His always somewhat irascible demeanor had been exacerbated since his diagnosis of Alzheimer's-related dementia, and I was never sure when I would get a call telling me that he'd lashed out at someone. As I readied my usual, "I'm so sorry," Alejandra instead said, "Don't worry, he's been good. His friend Al is here visiting him. They're out on the patio."

"Great," I said, and thought, *Ugh, Al.*

I dutifully walked out onto the back patio and found my dad sitting in his wheelchair under a tree with his friend — and former assistant chief at the police station — sitting next to him on the bench. My dad always had kind of a spark-plug build, but his increasingly grizzled appearance as he sat hunched over next to Al, who was a hulking 6'3" or so, made him look even smaller.

"Sam, it's good to see you," Al boomed, his voice matching his appearance.

"Good to see you, too, Al. It's nice of you to come and visit Dad." I meant the latter part. The first part, maybe not so much. Some of my dad's cop cronies could be a bit much. Al was particularly bombastic.

"Always happy to chew the fat with Chief Powers. You know that. Besides, I've got nothing but time ever since I 'took retirement,'" Al said, creating the air quotes with his fingers.

Carmel had a new, youngish — meaning middle-aged — police chief who, according to the local newspaper, had been cleaning house of the older cops, especially those from my dad's era. That, of course, included Al, who'd been there forever. While most of my dad's other cronies had already been phased out, Al received special treatment because he was handy and the station was showing its age. But they were finally getting a new station, so the chief decided it was Al's time to go as well and offered him a deal he couldn't refuse (as they say).

    I will admit Al looked good, and I could see it made Dad happy to sit shooting the breeze, even if it was mostly Al shooting the breeze and my dad smiling while listening to the stories. Who knows how many were getting through to him, but it was clear he enjoyed Al's company. Al slapped his back, and Dad got a grin on his face that I hadn't seen in a long time. I was glad. That didn't mean I wanted to hear Al's stories, so I excused myself and headed out.

    With my last excuse used up, I couldn't put off going home any longer. It's not that I was avoiding going home. Except that I was. And it's not that I didn't love the family home I had returned to following my dad's diagnosis. I loved that old house. Built by my great grandparents a century earlier, it was located on a gorgeous (and large by Carmel standards) spit of land near Carmel River State Beach. In those days, the area was considered the boondocks, based on the old black-and-white photograph of their groundbreaking we had hanging on the wall, where the land was surrounded by open space. While the lots around us had filled in with more modern houses, we still had the best view in town from our old-school Carmel stone-and-wood structure.

Chapter One

The house had undergone a lot of changes over the years, with additions by my grandparents and then my parents. This included separate wings in the main house, one for my dad and late mom, which we had closed off, and one for my Uncle Henry, plus a studio unit over the garage created by my dad when I was in high school, and I (and, heck, they) needed some space. I dropped my bag there before heading into the main house, taking a deep breath before opening the door.

I mean, I knew what I would find. It would be the usual tableau of Uncle Henry sitting by the fireplace with a cup of tea and his face in a book alongside his English bulldog, Buster, and my cat (yes, my cat in dog-loving Carmel) Stella. As adorable as the sight always was, lately it conjured a deep frustration within me.

It's not that I didn't love my Uncle Henry. Younger than my dad by quite a few years, he was smart, funny, and handsome. As lovable as they come. I was happy to share the family home with him. It's that, well, the house itself was starting to show its age. I don't mean the walls were falling down or the roof was caving in, although there was a pretty serious leak over the kitchen counter every time it rained. It was a lot of little stuff. Doors sticking, sinks backing up, heaters conking out, light fixtures failing, ants invading. In short, all the things anybody who owns an old house knows to expect to be fixing all the time, in addition to continually updating things like batteries in smoke alarms. Damn that chirp that always happens at 3 a.m.! Add in bigger problems like the potential of winter storms to undermine the exterior sewer line and they, well, they added up.

That was the issue. After my grandparents died, Dad was the fixer-upper in the family, so the house hadn't been worked on since he had the breakdown that precipitated his move into the assisted living facility that brought me home. And who knows what fixes were being made (or not) when no one noticed he was slowly losing his memory? While Uncle Henry and I both have a lot of positive qualities, they tend to be of the more cerebral variety. I mean, I'm a 35-year-old former investigative reporter turned travel writer who had always lived in apartments where I could just call the manager if there was a problem. And Henry's a 73-year-old legal brainiac teaching at the local law school. Neither of us is what you'd call "handy." With two equally inept people taking care of the place, who the hell was going to fix these things?

The worst part was that I seemed to be the only one noticing that everything was falling apart. Henry's mind was always somewhere else—either face in a book or, more recently, enjoying the occasional meal with Mona (yes, that Mona!). The place could literally be crumbling around him, and he was never going to notice. Our conversations had started following an increasingly enraging pattern.

"Henry, it's raining and the drip's back over the kitchen counter. Where did you put the pan?"
"Back in the cupboard, of course."

✦ Chapter One ✦

"Hey, Henry, did you notice we had no hot water this morning?"

"It was a little brisk, wasn't it?"

"Brisk? It was like small icicles pummeling my body."

"Did you check the recirculating pump?"

"What the hell is a recirculating pump?"

Or, the worst: "Henry, let me in!" That was me yelling and pounding on a front door that was stuck AGAIN. Sometimes, I had to walk around and tap on the window to get the attention of the possibly-going-deaf Buster, the dog, and Stella, the cat, for Henry to even look up from his book.

Thankfully, when I got home this time, the door didn't stick. Too much. I managed to wrestle it open on my first try, only to find that Henry was not sitting in his usual spot by the fireplace. Then I remembered it was Tuesday. He taught his class at the Monterey School of Law on Tuesday evenings. I found Buster and Stella sleeping nestled together near the fireplace in the sweetest way possible. They didn't even notice I was home until they heard the door close. Maybe they were both going deaf. Then I got the usual wet snout against the leg (Buster) while Stella winded her way through my legs in an attempt to kill me (in the most loving way possible, of course).

I patted their adorable heads, checked the mail, poured myself a glass of wine, and went outside to watch the sunset on the bench in the succulent garden my mother had created on our bluff overlooking the ocean. The sight of her plants coupled with the rolling waves usually managed to soothe me. Unfortunately, this time they weren't working their magic. For one, even though the calendar said it was spring, we had a thick layer of fog, the wind was whipping, and I could see some pretty wicked white caps. "The sea was angry that day, my friend" (as they say). The sea was decidedly angry. Fit my mood, I suppose.

It didn't help that looking out at the ocean also reminded me that I was 2,000 miles away from my kind-of boyfriend, Roger Kai, the Maui detective I'd met the previous year on my first press trip for the magazine—to the luxurious Mokihana Resort & Spa, no less. When one of the press trip participants (someone seemingly everyone loathed) dropped dead in a suspicious manner and I was the last person to see him alive, Roger and I were thrown together. And the more I got to know him, the more I, you know, liked him. A former military intelligence agent who kept his black hair short and wore aviator-style sunglasses, my first impression was of a total stick-in-the-mud. But take off those glasses and gaze into those warm brown eyes and the mud wasn't quite so sticky (hey, sue me, sometimes the metaphors don't totally work). Add to that the Hawaiian-style leather-and-bone bracelets he wore around his wrists and his days playing volleyball at UC Santa Barbara and surfing his home beaches of Maui, and they added up to a pretty dishy package. At least for me. And he seemed to feel the same—although he probably wouldn't use the word "dishy."

We had been seeing each other ever since that trip. In theory, at least. That's why he was still a "kind-of" boyfriend. We were limited to a lot of phone calls,

Chapter One

video chats, and a couple of in-person visits using his flight attendant sister's airline benefits—one when he came to visit me in Carmel for my birthday and another when he met me in Los Angeles as a final farewell to my old apartment down there. Both solidified the fact that I was crazy for the guy.

Mostly, we spent a lot of time talking on the phone, with me waving across the ocean at him, like I was about to do now.

"Hey there," I said, when he answered my video chat request.

"Hey yourself," he said, raising and lowering his eyebrows with a smile.

Swoon. But I was cool. "Whatcha doing?"

"Packing."

"Packing?"

"I'm attending the IFSA, remember?"

"IFSA?" I racked my brain, trying to remember what the hell it stood for.

"International Forensic Sciences Association. Cop convention."

"Oh, that's right." I had a vague memory of him telling me about it, but it was also when we were together at my old place in Venice Beach and let's just say I had other things on my mind (and lips and other body parts—you get the drift). "Where is it again?"

"The Midtown Hotel in New York."

Now I remembered why I'd blocked the trip from my brain. Roger mentioned the trip when I was in the throes of lust (sorry, I'll stop now), so when Mona told me about the plan for the magazine to cover the newly renovated Françoise Hotel, I had an all-too-brief glimpse into a fanciful tryst in New York City with a handsome Maui police detective. All of that was quashed when Mona said she was taking the trip herself. I couldn't blame her. She was the editor-in-chief and longtime family friend who got me the job that was taking me to some pretty amazing places, but still...

"Maybe you and Mona could have lunch while you are there," I said in my most petulant voice.

"Sam."

"Roger."

"You know how these things are. I'll be there with my boss, the police chief, so it will be 24 hours a day of cop talk, and you..."

"...hate cop talk," I ended his sentence for him. "I know. But to be in the same city as you for a short amount of time would be enough."

"We'll get another trip together soon. I promise."

"Pinky swear?"

"*I olelo mua ia'i.*"

"That sounds serious."

"I am serious." He used the tone of voice that got me, you know, kind of hot.

"I miss you." Okay, yeah, I said it.

"I miss you, too," he said. More radiating heat. "But I'm sure you can find something to occupy yourself with while I'm at the convention."

"Oh, there's plenty. This old house is falling apart."

"It is a pretty big house for you and Henry to take care of by yourself."

"Especially when Henry's way of helping is to walk to the library, check out books on plumbing and door repair, and leave them on the kitchen counter for me."

Chapter One

Roger laughed. Oh, I liked that laugh. But it just brought more pain. "Don't laugh. Ever heard of a recirculating pump?"

"Not something they cover at the IFSA."

"According to Henry's books, I need one of those and something called a strike plate for the door."

"Maybe it's time to hire a professional."

"We don't have the money."

And therein lay the irony. Our location on that large spit of land with one of the nicest views in Carmel, coupled with a recent spike in real estate prices, meant our old barn of a house was starting to be worth a lot of money. I won't lie and say it hadn't occurred to me that the money we'd make if we sold it could easily take care of the three of us—five if you included the animals—quite nicely for the rest of our lives. But where would we go and what about the house? The house that meant so much to my family for so many years? As I sat looking out at the succulent garden my mom had so lovingly tended, the thought of losing it broke my heart. But so did the thought of dealing with—not to mention paying for—the constant upkeep.

As I ended the call, I looked out across the sea in the direction of the man I couldn't be with while saddled with the responsibilities of a sick dad and a house that was falling apart. As if to prove my point, I even noted some grassy weeds poking their way through my mom's succulent garden. With no signs of relief or even the slightest glimpse of adventure in the near future, I felt trapped and alone.

CHAPTER TWO

*E*arly the following morning, my phone rang at the god-awful hour of 5 a.m. I let it go to voicemail, cursing myself that I hadn't enabled "do not disturb" like I usually do before going to bed. When the damn thing started ringing again not two seconds later, I pressed "accept" and grunted something—who the hell knows what—into the small device that brings us such convenience and annoyance all in one package.

That's when I heard the words: "Sam, I need your help."

"Huh?" I managed.

"Sam, Sam, are you there?"

In my sleep-groggled (not a word, but it should be, right?) state, I could make out that the voice was Mona's. I squinted and saw her name on the phone to match the voice.

"Mona?"

Chapter Two

"Oh, god, I woke you up, didn't I?"

"No. Of course not," I totally lied.

"I forgot the three-hour time difference."

Now I knew something was up. Mona? Forget, well, anything?

"What's up, Mona?"

"It's a mess, Sam."

"What's a mess?"

"Everything. This conference. Maxine's conference. The Françoise."

"The Françoise?"

"The hotel. That's the hotel, Sam."

"Got it." But did I? Not really. "How can I help?" By this point, I was sitting up.

"Can you come out?"

"Where?"

"New York. I need you to join me in New York. I've already made your airplane reservations. You just have to get to the Monterey airport by 10:35 a.m. Can you do that?"

Now I knew something was up. I looked at the time again. That gave me about five hours. "I guess."

"Great. I'll text you the details and fill you in when you get here," Mona said. "And dress appropriately. You're coming to New York, for god's sake." There she was: the Mona I knew and loved. "Oh, and thank Henry for his advice."

Uncle Henry? What the hell was going on?

I showered and started throwing some things in a bag. I scoured my closet for "New York" appropriate clothing items, mostly tossing in everything I had that was black. A quick scan of the weather (much warmer than Carmel!) led me to add some cotton skirts from my L.A. days. For good measure, I threw in a few scarves Mona had given me as gifts. You know, in case I was invited somewhere fancy. That would have to do until I had some coffee and could think straight.

I made my way over to the main house, using my shoulder to punch my way through the front door. First try. Not bad, although my left shoulder was starting to feel a little tender. As I entered the living area, I could see the sun starting to rise in the hills behind the house as the last remnants of the moon set over the ocean. It really was beautiful and I felt guilty for even pondering the idea of selling the place. Between that guilt and Mona's strange early morning call, my frustration with Uncle Henry had lessened by the time I reached the kitchen. I was happy to see that he was already up and had made a pot of coffee. I found him sitting at the currently leak-free kitchen counter reading the newspaper. Yes, he still picked it up every morning like the true Luddite that he was. He looked as dapper as always, with his more-salt-than-pepper hair, tall, lean physique (total opposite of my dad's), and always well-pressed clothes.

"Morning, Uncle Henry."

"Samantha."

"How was class?" I said, pouring coffee into my cup.

Henry looked up from the paper. "What's wrong?"

Chapter Two

I looked back and saw him staring at me. "What do you mean?"

"I think 'what's wrong?' is pretty self-explanatory."

"How do you do that?"

"What?"

"Know when something's up."

Henry shrugged. "You're deflecting."

"Mona called."

That got his attention. He nodded. "Oh, yes. Of course."

"She said she'd talked to you."

"Yes, last night as I was returning from class."

"She wants me to join her in New York. Said something about things being a mess."

"Yes. I suggested your presence might be beneficial."

"Do you know what's up?"

"She could use your help with the conference."

"In what way? If it's magazine-related, wouldn't our sales manager Stacy or even Chelsea or Katie be more appropriate?"

"No. I think you're the best fit and I think she should be the one to tell you."

That was cryptic as hell, but it gave me an opening. "So... Uncle Henry... What's up with you two?"

"Meaning?"

"Meaning you and Mona have been seeing each other a lot lately."

"That is true."

"Are you upset she went to New York?"

"Why would I be?"

"I don't know. New lady love hitting the Big Apple without you."

Henry looked at me over his readers. "Mona is not new to me, Sam. We have known each other for most of our lives."

"I know, but it's only recently you've been 'hanging out.'" I didn't use Al's air quotes but I did give "hanging out" a little extra emphasis.

Henry smiled, despite himself. "We enjoy each other's company. She's a neat lady."

Neat lady? I decided to let it go. For now. Instead, I said, "I saw Dad yesterday."

"How's he doing?"

"Hasn't hit anybody recently, so I took that as a win. His old cop friend Al Castro was there."

"Good old Al. How's he doing?"

"Good. Retired. Doesn't seem too happy about it."

"Understandable." He took another sip of his coffee. "Nice for your dad to have more visitors."

"Al was chatting away and Dad was actually smiling."

"Smiling? That is a good thing. I hope it continues."

"Me, too," I said. "So, you will visit him while I'm in New York?"

"You know I will."

"Thanks, Uncle Henry."

Henry put his nose back into the newspaper. I looked at the library books on plumbing and door repair on the counter and briefly considered broaching the topic of the house repairs. Instead, in true Powers fashion, I just pushed the books in his direction before saying, "I better go finish packing if I'm going to make my flight."

✶ Chapter Two ✶

"Be safe, Sam. And call if you need anything." He looked back at me. "I mean anything."

"You know I will."

I gave him a kiss on the cheek, grabbed one of the pastries he'd picked up from Carmel Bakery on his early morning walk to pick up the paper, and went back to my studio to finish packing.

Two flights and a train from the airport later, I made my way out of Penn Station and took a moment to acclimate to the noise. So much noise. And yelling. And honking. Why did everybody seem to be so mad at each other? And why were there so many of them? I found a spot against a wall where I wouldn't get jostled and looked at the address Mona had texted me while I was traveling. Based on the spot on the map that opened up, it was not The Françoise Hotel, which I knew was on 5th Avenue next to Central Park. The little blue ball on the map identified a spot on 38th Street between Park and Madison avenues. That didn't look all that far away from where I stood at 34th and 7th — three long blocks across and then five shorter ones up. Walkable, right?

As I started out, lugging my carry-on behind me over the bumps in the sidewalk and through the hordes of people, I thought about how different — and yet the same — this walk was from the one I'd taken just the day before in Carmel. Was I complaining about "crowds" in Carmel? And was that just the day before? Travel really screws with the sense of time.

Bump bump bump, wait for the light, bump bump bump, wait for the light. Avoid the bikes flying by as you start into the intersection. Okay, I got this, I thought.

Although it was already well into the evening, the spring temperatures were warmer and muggier than I was used to. The more I walked, the more I started to sweat. *No biggie,* I kept thinking. Just four (then three, then two) more blocks. I stripped off my jacket and tied it around my waist as I doggedly continued making my way through the city, determined to make it to what the map told me was the Murray Hill neighborhood. Finally, I reached a block of low-rise buildings—at least by NYC standards, meaning all were maybe 3-5 stories. In the middle, was a large reddish-brown building wedged between two narrower buildings, one white stone, one red brick. The brown building had a half dozen steps leading up to a bright red door with a sign to the side that said "Tina's Dance Studio" above a black rectangle with a keypad on it.

I pressed the "home" button at the top of the keypad and heard a voice say, "Hello?" I started to say, "Hi, this is Sam…" but before I could get the rest out, heard a buzz and then a click that meant the door had unlocked. I pushed the door and found a small vestibule with a second door that was also buzzing. I quickly opened that door before the buzzing stopped and found myself in the entryway of the apartment (or, I guess, townhouse?). The wide hallway featured a series of benches with cubbyholes for shoes below hooks for jackets before opening up to what had probably once been a grand living room or even ballroom,

Chapter Two

with huge walls and gorgeous high ceilings now framed by mirrors and a ballet bar. "We're back here," I heard a voice say from behind a stairway.

I followed the voice past a door and through a smaller hall, which led me into an expansive living area. In the back by floor-to-ceiling windows, a dozen people sat around a dining room table. I'm not sure what I expected, but similar to the cacophony of sounds found in the street, the first thing I noticed was auditory: clinking glasses and silverware, loud voices, and laughter. Raucous laughter.

CHAPTER THREE

"Samantha! You made it!" Mona said, standing up at the far end of the dining room table as everyone turned to look at me. "You have to meet everyone. Everyone, this is Sam."

Wishing I'd thought to stop in a bathroom at the airport or train station to freshen up, I gave a meek little wave to the group assembled before me while also attempting to pat the sweat off my face and pull my auburn curls into a semblance of order. The people at the table ranged in age from two who looked right out of college to a man who looked older than Uncle Henry, like a lot older. Their dress style was also all over the place, from business suits to artsy bohemian garb. Still others were dressed like Mona (in other words, absolutely fabulous).

Chapter Three

A tiny sprig of a woman with long silver hair pulled into a bun held together with a chopstick followed Mona over to greet me.

"Samantha!" she said. "I'm so happy to finally meet you."

Before I knew it, the woman enveloped me in a hug. "Sam, this is Tina," said Mona, looming behind her. "Tina runs a dance academy, as well as something of a boarding house for dancers and other young people new to the city, here in her brownstone."

Brownstone! That's what they're called. Duh.

"Cool."

"Cool, indeed," said Tina, laughing. "And yes, the most adorable youngsters seem to end up on my doorstep. Including this one, 40 years ago." Tina gave Mona's elbow a hug, which was the best she could do given their height difference.

"Oh, that makes me sound so old," Mona said, laughing. "I was, of course, five at the time."

"You wanted to be a dancer?" I asked.

"No, thank god," Mona said. "Your mother's friend Gayle…"

"Mom's flower shop partner Gayle?"

"Yes," Mona said, sharply and with a look that said to stop interrupting her. "Gayle and Tina grew up together, so when I told your mom I was moving to New York to look for a job at a fashion magazine, she recommended I contact Tina."

"I am the California connection," Tina said with a curtsy.

"I suppose that makes me the latest," I said, looking around at the immense space. "I forget there are, like, real houses here in New York. This is great."

"Thank you," said Tina. "My husband and I were lucky enough to come into some money back in the late 1970s when he received a commission to create a sculpture for a financial firm down on Wall Street. In those days, New York City was supposedly dying and real estate prices were dirt cheap, so we were able to get the place for almost nothing." Tina looked around with a smile. "It was a dump, of course. Ripe for a total reno. So—with help from some wildly creative friends and additional money from a relative of mine who believed in our vision—we transformed the front room into the dance studio, turned the top floor into our digs, and rented out the bedrooms on the second floor to dancers and actors and other creative types. Or young fashionistas like Mona."

Tina gave Mona another little elbow hug and Mona smiled.

"And Maxine, of course. My little M&Ms, I used to call them."

Mona's smile dimmed just a bit.

"That's so cool," I again said, realizing I might need to step up my vocabulary at some point.

Tina laughed. "It was a mess, of course. Still is, in a lot of ways—but my husband was very handy, and we had a lot of helpful friends, so we were able to keep it up ourselves."

"Sounds like my family's house in Carmel," I said.

"Then you know that these old places can be a blessing and a curse," Tina said, laughing.

Chapter Three

"I very much understand," I said. "Maybe you can give me some tips on how to take care of it."

Tina leaned in conspiratorially. "Ask for help," she said. "And make it a party." Tina laughed. "Actually, my nephew is the one you should talk to. He's a stagehand on Broadway and has been a godsend since my husband died. Don't worry, I'm sure you'll meet him. He lives in the basement apartment." Tina started moving us toward the table. "Until then, come and join us. We've gathered to try to figure out how to handle the Maxine situation."

"Maxine situation?"

"Oh, you haven't heard?" Tina said.

"I haven't completely filled her in," Mona said, turning to me. "That's why I wanted you to come out, Sam. Maxine, well, she's disappeared."

"Disappeared?"

Mona shrugged. "She's gone."

"Gone?"

"Samantha, if you're just going to repeat everything I say..." Mona started.

"Don't be so hard on the poor girl, Mona. It is a bit of a shock, even if she doesn't know Maxine."

"Lucky her," said one of the table guests, an impeccably dressed woman with caramel-colored skin, black hair kept very short, and bright red eyeglasses. All eyes turned in her direction, including the youngsters at the table, who appeared to be as enthralled as I was with the conversation.

"Scarlet!" said Tina.

"Oh, let's not pretend Maxine is a saint," the now-named Scarlet said. The bald man sitting next to her, who had a well-trimmed beard and appeared to be her husband (based on their matching wedding bands and expensive-looking eyeglasses) nodded.

"Or that this is the first time she's gone AWOL," added the older man, who had a melodic voice tinged with a British accent.

Scarlet gave a small snort. Oh, I liked these people.

"It is Maxine's world, and we are mere players in it," the older man continued.

"Shakespeare?" Mona asked.

He nodded. "*As You Like It*, although in Maxine's case, the scenario has always skewed more toward tragedy than comedy."

I wasn't sure what he meant by that.

"Maxine ... has always had some demons," Mona said quietly.

"I suppose that's what you could call twelve 'spa' visits," and, yes, he used the air quotes (I was starting to notice just how often people used the damn things), "in the past four years."

"Winston..." Tina started.

"I thought she called it 'going to the Hamptons,'" said Scarlet.

"To only the best and most expensive 'spas' in the Hamptons, of course," said the now-named Winston.

I felt really thick as I attempted to figure out what code they were speaking when Mona whispered, "Rehab, Sam, darling. She goes to rehab."

"Maxine likes her high-end vodka," said Winston.

"A lot," Scarlet emphasized.

"Dry, dirty Bonheur vodka martini up with three olives," they all said in unison.

* Chapter Three *

"I thought she liked Laporte vodka?" Mona said.

"No, she's a Bonheur gal all the way. Ever since her marriage to Pierre, the French race car driver."

"And she insists on eating one olive before the first sip."

"To create a base, darling," Winston said, in an exaggerated, snobby American accent.

"Of course."

"And then she disappears and someone finds her sitting in her apartment surrounded by bottles of generic vodka."

"We know she's on a bender when she's drinking the cheap stuff."

"Then it's off to the 'spa in the Hamptons, darlings.'"

"And then things are fine for a while," said Winston.

"And then they aren't."

"And now they aren't," Mona said. "Or we really don't know, do we?"

"We don't," Tina agreed. "Usually, we know when she's checked herself in somewhere to get cleaned up or can at least reach her by phone."

"No phone?" I asked.

"It goes straight to voicemail, as if it's been turned off. She seems to have fallen off the face of the earth," Mona said. "That's why I called you, Sam. I'm hoping you might help us try to find her before the conference."

Moi? "When does it start?"

"In two days."

"Two days? You're not going to cancel?"

"Oh, the conference will go on no matter what," Mona said.

"It's what Maxine would want," Tina said, with the rest of the people at the table nodding.

"That conference is her lifeblood," said Mona. "And important to a lot of people."

"It is all set."

"Plus, Harriet knows what to do…"

"Harriet?" I asked, looking around the table to see if one of them was Harriet.

"Maxine's chief operating officer," Mona explained. "She's been running the logistics of the conference for years. Maxine's more the content provider. That's already set, and Harriet's over at The Françoise now with the rest of the show team. Don't worry, you'll meet them all tomorrow."

"And in the meantime, please sit down and have something to eat," Tina said. "You must be starving after that long plane ride."

I sat down at the table and started to eat from a hodgepodge of dishes that indicated the meal had been a potluck. Tina wasn't wrong that the long day of traveling made me hungry! While I ate, I started cataloging the cast of characters around the table, giving the ones whose names I caught a nickname, which was the only way I knew how to remember them. The two youngsters appeared to be the latest incoming residents of the brownstone and ranged from bright-eyed (Naïve Natalie) to somewhat goth-like (Emo Emily). Emo Emily had the remnants of a cake in front of her, saying "Welcome to the family." I wondered if Tina did that for every new tenant.

The older ones were obviously longtime friends of Tina—and Mona and the elusive Maxine. Winston,

✦ Chapter Three ✦

the gentleman with the melodic voice, was indeed an actor. Although he most recently had appeared as a servant—head butler, in fact—on one of those costume dramas on PBS, I decided to call him Sir Winston. Give him a promotion, as it were. Scarlet, I learned, served as the chief financial officer for a big publishing house as well as Tina's accountant. I'd call her Spreadsheet Scarlet. Her husband, an art gallery owner who hardly spoke a word—mostly sitting with a bemused grin on his face—was named Victor. I think the style of beard he wore was called a Van Dyke so I called him Victor Van Dyke.

To say they were entertaining was an understatement. Tina, Mona, Winston, and Scarlet, especially, volleyed words back and forth like the balls in one of Lizzy's tennis matches from when she played on the pro circuit. I joined the others in swiveling our heads back and forth in response.

"Welcome to New York, Samantha," said Winston, suddenly sending the ball in my direction (as it were). "I'm sure everyone has warned you to look out for the rats."

"Of the human or vermin variety?" I asked.

"I like her," Victor said quietly, the first words I'd heard him utter all evening.

Well, look at me, fitting in with the New Yorkers! I thought. I found myself smiling when I heard the buzz in my pocket that meant a text had come in. Actually, quite a few, mostly from Henry and Lizzy, who in all my travel angst I had forgotten to tell I arrived safe and sound. I remedied that and noticed that I still had the "Safe travels!" message from Roger in response to the text I sent before I left to let him know I was coming to New York after all. I sent him a "Made it to the city!" message along with a happy face emoji as well.

It was after 11—still only 8 p.m. my time—when Tina's guests started peeling off after helping to cart the leftover food and dishes into the kitchen. The youngsters headed upstairs to their rooms and the elders to wherever they lived. Mona gave me a hug and said that Tina had a room for me to stay in at the brownstone, and she would see me the following morning at The Françoise Hotel.

"The time difference can be rough the first morning, so come by whenever you wake up, and we'll get you some coffee and breakfast," Mona said.

"Thanks, Mona, I appreciate it," I said, as the others left through the front door.

"Here, let me show you to your room," Tina said, grabbing my carry-on. Instead of taking me upstairs, she walked me back past the dining room and through a large kitchen, where an immense pile of dishes had been stacked in the sink.

"Can I help you with these?" I asked, pointing to the sink.

"No, don't worry about it. We'll get it all later," Tina said before reaching a small room at the back of the kitchen. She opened the door.

"This is where Mimi usually stays, but she's been on the road for the past six months. She's a dancer in the 8,000[th] production of *Hamilton*." Tina smiled. "I may be embellishing a bit, but there are a lot of

Chapter Three

productions going on around the world, and thank god for my students they need a lot of dancers."

As I got closer, I could see that the room was about the size of my mom's walk-in closet back home. Was there more beyond the door that I couldn't see? Nope.

"I know it's small," Tina said, noting my wide eyes. "In the 1800s, when this brownstone was built, it would have been the maid's quarters. But, as you can see, it has a bathroom connected, so really you have everything you need." Tina's chipper tone didn't quite overcome the visuals.

Tina turned and gave me another quick hug. "I'm so happy to finally meet you, Samantha, especially after everything Mona has told us." Before I could ask what that might be, she slipped back out through the kitchen and was gone.

I pulled my bag into the room. Even though it was a carry-on, I could barely squeeze it by the twin bed and had to use the end of the bed to open it up. The gal who lived here obviously lived very lightly to have everything she needed in this room, although I discovered some handy built-ins under the bed. I also noted the walls were filled with pictures of happy dancers, each with a date and a note of gratitude to Tina. That was sweet, even if none of them mentioned living in a closet.

As I looked for a wall socket to plug in my phone, I finally saw a message from Roger: "Glad you made it in safely. Headed to bed after a long day. Let's touch base tomorrow." I had to admit that I would have liked a little more excitement at the fact we were both in New York City. Before I could wallow further, the phone buzzed again: Lizzy.

"Hey, Lizzy," I answered.

"How is it, big city girl?"

"Well, at the moment, this big city girl is in a room the size of a closet in the house of one of Mona's friends. Everyone else has gone to bed."

"It is 11:30 out there, right?"

"Yeah, but it's only 8:30 California time," I whined.

"Is Roger happy you're there?"

"No. I don't know. All I got was a cryptic text that he'd had a long day and was going to bed."

"Understandable."

"Oh, come on, Lizzy. It's only 5:30 Hawaii time." More whining.

"Didn't he have a killer 10-hour flight from Hawaii…"

"Thirteen hours, including the layover."

"…and a full day at a conference?"

"With his boss, the police chief."

"He's there with his boss? Oh my god, Sam. Of course, he's exhausted."

"I know. I just had this fantasy…"

"That's all it is, Sam. Total fantasy. This is real life and a guy who's shown that he's crazy about you by coming to visit you twice. Let it go."

"But it's supposed to be the city that never sleeps," I whined just a little more.

"Most of us humans need the stuff, Sam. Go to bed."

I hung up the phone, pulled out my toothbrush and was heading to the sink in the phone-booth-sized bathroom when I heard rustling in the kitchen. Still not tired at all and thinking I could again offer to

Chapter Three

help Tina with the dishes, I opened the door to find a tall, blond, and built (sue me, that's what I noticed first) man who looked to be in his late 30s or early 40s rummaging through the refrigerator. He turned in my direction when he saw the door open.

"Hey Meem…" he started. "Oh, you're not Mimi."

"No, I'm Sam. Samantha Powers."

He still looked confused.

"Mona's friend from California."

A little less confused but still confused.

"Tina's friend Mona. Mid-60s, used to be a *Vogue* editor, really tall, now back living in Carmel."

He nodded. "Got it," he said with a smile. A really nice smile. "As you might imagine, the number of people coming through Aunt Tina's sometimes makes it hard to sort through them all, but Mona the tall *Vogue* editor who moved back to California I remember."

"I am guessing you're the nephew."

"In the flesh," he said with a smile and a curtsy just like his aunt. Adorable. "I'm Hastings, and before you ask, it's an old family name. I was named after the relative who helped Aunt Tina pay for the renovation of this brownstone half a century ago. Not sure if it was dictated in the will or just a nice gesture, but I'm stuck with it."

I wasn't going to ask about his name, although I appreciated the explanation. He just became Hunky Hastings to me. Man, he was gorgeous. Purely aesthetically speaking, of course, and partly because it appeared (at least on the surface) that he didn't realize just how good-looking he was, with his soft features, wavy blond hair that had never seen a drop of mousse, and sapphire blue eyes.

"There's usually no one up by the time I get home from the theater," Hastings said.

"I'm still on California time," I said.

"That explains it, then," he said. "And what brings you out?"

"I guess I'm here to help with Maxine's conference or, I suppose, help find Maxine…"

"Maxine, I know," he said with a sigh. "She's gone AWOL again?"

"Apparently, and not to any of her usual spots, from what I gathered from the group."

"The group. Ah, hence all the extra food," he said, pointing to the leftover foodstuffs he was currently arranging into a meal. "Aunt Tina always convenes her round table when Maxine's causing trouble. I can usually guess who was here, based on what they bring." He looked over the various food items. "Let me guess: Winston," pointing to a container with a Myers of Kenswick logo on the side, "and Victor and Scarlet," pointing to one with a Zabar's logo, "were among the participants."

"I think so," I said, although from what I could remember, he was pretty spot on. "I didn't get a lot of time with them and have never been the best at names."

"And you're, what, a detective?"

I laughed. "Me? Hardly. I'm the travel columnist for Mona's magazine. Although I used to work as an investigative reporter and my dad was the police chief back in Carmel, so I suppose Mona thought I

Chapter Three

could help. Truth be told, I'm really not sure why she wants me here."

Hastings pondered the information as he took a seat at a very well-loved kitchen nook. He pointed to a seat across the table. "I'd love the company, if you're so inclined. Otherwise, it's just me and the resident mouse."

While pushing the idea of a resident mouse out of my head as much as possible (and noting a box labeled non-toxic rat poison on top of the refrigerator), I briefly debated whether getting to know this gorgeous hunk of a man was better than staring up at the ceiling in the closet they called my room. No, I jest. I didn't ponder it at all. "I'd be happy to join you."

I took a seat on the bench across the table from him as he poured us each a glass of wine from one of the bottles left over from his aunt's "round table." For the record, I'm quoting him here, not air quoting.

"So, I hear you're handy with a wrench," I said, in what is quite possibly the worst opening line ever uttered by a human being. "Oh, god, I'm so sorry," I said, backtracking desperately and laughing at my own idiocy. "Your aunt said you were very helpful with the brownstone. As it happens, I'm dealing with an old family house that's falling apart back in Carmel and somehow those are the words that came out of my mouth."

Hastings grinned. "Understood. And, yes, I help Aunt Tina keep the place going. In exchange, I get the basement apartment and whatever food is left over after one of her soirees," he said, indicating the feast in front of him.

"She has a lot of them?"

"Tina loves bringing people together."

Like us, I suppose, I thought. "She mentioned you work on Broadway?"

"I do. I'm the assistant technical supervisor for one of the Disney extravaganzas at the Palazzo Theatre, but I also help out at some off-off Broadway houses and with art installations at Victor's gallery."

"Fun."

"Can be."

"You know, I have never been to a Broadway show."

"We might have to remedy that, don't you think? We sometimes have house seats available at the last minute. I'd be happy to text you if that happens while you're still here."

"I'd like that."

Hastings smiled and I realized I already liked New York quite a bit.

CHAPTER FOUR

Mona was right that the three-hour time difference made the following morning a killer. The sun started coming through the small window above my bed after 6 a.m., a.k.a. 3 a.m. California time. The songs of the birds (the first time I'd heard them!) and then the rest of the city awakening followed, along with what sounded like voices—or was that the scurrying of little feet?—coming through the exposed pipes in the bathroom just a few feet away.

I tied a sweater around my head to cover my eyes and ears to see if I could grab another couple of hours' sleep, especially since I hadn't finished chatting with Hastings until after 1 a.m. As I fell back asleep, images of the group at the table discussing the mysterious Maxine morphed into a long hall where I was following someone in a red coat who kept turning and disappearing every time I got to the same corner.

Suddenly, the people at the dinner kept appearing, as did Hunky Hastings, who leaned in for a kiss before turning into Roger. Yikes. That woke me up with a jolt. *What the fuck?*

I checked my phone. I'd made it to 7:30. A modicum of successful sleep, I suppose, even if I was still a little (okay, a lot) groggy. It occurred to me it had been less than 24 hours since Mona first called me in Carmel. Crazy. I managed to take a shower in the oh-so-tiny bathroom, which doubled as a closet. Really, there was a rod to hang clothes on to go along with the exposed pipes for the plumbing. As Tina said, everything I needed was there, but man oh man was it minuscule. That might work for her tiny frame—yes, Tiny Tina was my nickname for her—or the dancer that lived there, but at 5'7", I needed to do some ducking to make things work while also worrying about what furry creatures might be crawling behind those pipes.

I grabbed an outfit from my carry-on that I hoped was appropriate attire for visiting The Françoise Hotel: black pants and a dark gray blouse. I only had sneakers and sandals. Do people own more than that? The sneakers were black, so I went with them and made up for my lack of fashionable footwear by adding a scarf Mona had given me for my birthday. I couldn't see what I looked like in the tiny mirror, but figured it would have to do.

I wasn't sure how long I would be staying at Tina's or if Mona had some other digs in mind, so I put everything back into my carry-on and left it sitting at the foot of the bed. As I did, I looked out the

Chapter Four

small window to see what the view was. Mostly just the building across the way. Looking down, I spotted some potted plants in a small alley.

After checking my phone for messages and finding none, I made my way out through the kitchen. I noticed that the dishes had miraculously all been done. I'm not sure how I didn't hear that, but even my brief encounter with Tiny Tina made her seem capable of more than a few feats of Mary Poppins-style magic. Maybe her nickname should be Tinker Bell Tina. Or perhaps the kids she rented the rooms to were in charge of the dishes, although I felt like they would have made some noise. As I made my way through the living area, I gave a wave to Naïve Natalie, who appeared to be rehearsing a scene with a friend. I then snuck past a dance class already in session in the front hall—wow, they were limber—headed out the front door, and down the stairs to the sidewalk.

Hello, New York City! I thought briefly, before a woman pushing a stroller almost plowed into me. She then gave me the evil eye for daring to stand still on the sidewalk, as did the dog she had following close behind. No, really, I swear the dog turned and glared. Jumping back up on the stairs to the brownstone, I opened the map feature on my phone to make sure I was going in the right direction.

I then looked both ways to make sure pedestrian merging would be possible and started walking west to Madison Avenue, where I caught the uptown bus, as Tina had directed. Well, I did on my second try. There were so many different signs on the street, it was hard to figure out where to stand and which bus would take me the 25 blocks north that I needed to go. After the first bus passed me by, two people got into place about 100 yards away from me. I joined them just as the next bus was arriving. Whew!

I made my way onto the bus—astonished that Tina's instructions to wave my phone at the meter to have the fare deducted from the credit card in my electronic wallet actually worked—and took a seat. The bus was quite the experience, I have to say. It felt like a microcosm of the city with people representing every demographic I could think of. Like the rest of New York, it was also rather loud, mostly because a grumpy older man got on the bus holding three plastic bags of groceries, announced to everyone assembled that he was having a bad day, and then loudly yelled "mooooove" at every car that dared drive into the bus lane in front of us. Not unlike the constant honking of horns, I wondered if the yelling really helped move things along.

As I sat in my seat, I felt a text come in. Roger. Finally.

"Hey Sam, we have a packed schedule today, so I'm not sure I'll be able to slip away. I hope you're enjoying your first day in NYC!"

This time he added a happy face with heart eyes emoji, but it didn't help. Come on, man, we were maybe a mile apart—you couldn't work a little harder to see me?

When the bus reached the 63rd Street stop, I got off and walked west toward Central Park. Now that it was daytime, I was able to get a closer look at my surroundings. Mostly, I found concrete: sidewalks

★ Chapter Four ★

and streets and buildings. So many buildings. On Madison, they were huge. Instead of the low-rise structures and cute little fairy-tale cottages of Carmel's business district, these were real New York skyscrapers. Every once in a while, on side streets like Tina's, I'd come upon similar brownstones, either a whole block of them together or sandwiched between humongous buildings. Based on signs and what I could see through the windows, a lot of them offered businesses on the ground floor—hair salons, doctors, daycare centers, dog groomers, psychics, Greek Orthodox Ladies Philoptochos Society (really, it's a thing)—with apartments or private clubs or who knows what else above. Each building seemed to offer so many possibilities. What was going on behind the doors? Home? Business? Artistic endeavor? Nefarious artistic endeavor? It could be anything! With Carmel, you could tell exactly what each building held, but here… everything was locked behind brick, cement, or steel façades. And so many of them! And so many people running in and out of them.

Where are they going? Who knows! Just don't get in their way!

Once I turned onto the block off Madison that would take me to The Françoise Hotel, I took a closer look at the buildings. I found a restaurant on the ground floor of a tall modern building next to an older white building with a set of stairs leading up to what looked like a grand mansion. There was a plaque on the doors that I couldn't quite read and what looked to be a pineapple carved into the door. A pineapple? Huh.

Finally, I found a bright green awning that said "The Françoise." The attached building was tall but not skyscraper tall. Maybe a dozen stories with a red brick façade that reeked of old and historic but with shiny doors that said "fixed up and fancy." Because it was all I could think about lately, I wondered if their maintenance people had any tips for our old house back in Carmel. I flashed on my question to Hastings and then to the strange dream I had just before I woke up that I found so troubling. *Shake it off, Sam. Shake it off.*

I walked through the revolving glass doors and was greeted by a well-appointed lobby with high ceilings and a tall man wearing a top hat and tuxedo. It was definitely a look I didn't see in Carmel, where casual wear is the norm, and (fun fact) there's still a law on the books that women need a permit to wear heels over two inches.

"May I help you, ma'am?" the man, whose nametag identified him as Renaldo, asked.

Ma'am? Ma'am? I took it in stride. "I'm here to meet Mona Reynolds," I said.

"Allow me to call up to her room," he said. "May I say who's calling?"

"Samantha Powers," I offered. "Mona said if she wasn't in her room, she might be in something called the show office?"

"For the Business of Luxury event?"

"Yes."

"Let's try her room first." The newly monikered Top Hat Renaldo smiled and walked me over to the concierge desk where a tall, impeccably dressed Black man who looked like the concierge in the *John*

Chapter Four

Wick movies appeared to be helping a couple with theater tickets. He managed to give me a small nod while not breaking stride in his instructions to the couple. As I nodded in return, I noticed the portrait of a man hanging on the wall behind him. The painting appeared to be quite old. On the bottom of the frame was a small plaque that read, "Reginald Wentworth" and then "Discretion Is Our Middle Name." Fancy.

While Renaldo spoke on the house phone, I backed away from the desk and took in more of the lobby. The painted ceiling looked like it belonged in an Italian palazzo, as did a gorgeous chandelier that brought my eye down to a sumptuous carpet that echoed the colors of the ceiling. The lobby itself wasn't massive but included a few couches and coffee tables, most of which were positioned next to a currently closed cocktail lounge on the left. Past the lounge entrance was the front desk. Put together, the entry created a feeling of warmth and history along with elegance and modernity. *Quite exquisite*, I thought, before remembering I wasn't writing about it. Mona was.

Amid all the glamour of the lobby, I again took stock of my outfit. It felt perfectly presentable when I left Tina's, but now I felt underdressed. I adjusted my scarf to make myself look a tad more formal. I mean, I didn't even own any heels above two inches.

"Ms. Reynolds is still in her room and asked that I send you up," I heard Top Hat Renaldo say right behind me. I jumped.

"Sorry. I didn't hear you come up," I said.

"Soft carpet," he said, smiling.

"Quite soft."

"Ms. Reynolds is in room 734. Allow me to show you the way."

Renaldo walked me to the far end of the lobby and then down the equally well-appointed hall to a series of three elevators, one of which had an attendant waiting outside — an attendant!!

"Leonora," Top Hat Renaldo said to the attendant, "Ms. Powers wishes to go to the 7th floor." *How fancy is that?*

"It would be my pleasure," said the elevator attendant, the aforementioned Leonora, now Levitating Leonora, of course.

Leonora, who had curly gray hair and a warm smile, wore a well-pressed white shirt under a black vest and gloved hands that she used to slide the outer gates of the elevator together. The inner automatic doors then closed, and we started up. The elevator didn't look like it had been updated in a hundred years, although the smooth ride meant that it most likely had. Above the door, a bronze half-moon-style dial indicated the floor levels. They started with a B on the left, then numbers 1-9, and a PH on the right. When the dial hit 7, the doors opened, and Leonora pulled back the outer gates to allow me to exit.

"Thank you, Leonora."

"It has been my pleasure, Ms. Powers."

So formal, these New Yorkers! At least the New Yorkers at The Françoise. Not sure how they fit in with Tina's bunch over at the brownstone, but I didn't have too long to ponder as I immediately saw Mona standing in one of the doorways down the hall.

✦ Chapter Four ✦

"Samantha," Mona said. "I see you've finally joined the land of the living."

"I have," I said. "You were right about the time difference making the first morning difficult. Yikes."

"Yikes indeed," said Mona, in a voice that said "yikes" wasn't a word she used, well, ever. But she did smile. "Come inside. I had some coffee sent up."

"Bless you."

I walked into her room—suite, actually. It was immense. Just immense. The little closet where I'd spent the night would fit in the hallway leading into the living area.

"Wow," I said. "This is amazing."

"They did a wonderful job with the renovation, don't you think?"

"I do think. And this room is huge."

"Suite. They were nice enough to give me a suite. Perhaps because I'm covering it for the magazine as well as speaking at the conference."

"It's because you're you, Mona."

"That's very sweet, dear, but I highly doubt that," she said, smiling as she handed me a cup of coffee. I took a sip, and it was goooood (but of course, right?). I might have moaned.

"Is it okay if I check it all out?"

"Of course," Mona said, turning her attention back to the laptop she had set up on the small desk in the living area. Oh yeah, her suite had a desk and a dining table and a couch and a humongous flat-screen television. I took another sip of my coffee and felt the caffeine begin to do its magic while I walked through to check out the rest of the place. Beautiful bedroom with a glistening duvet indicating a high thread count. Check. Sumptuous bathroom with a jetted tub and a steam shower. Check. Beautifully landscaped patio. Checkeroonie.

"Oh my god, look at this view!" I called from the patio. If I leaned over the banister and looked to the left, I could even see a speck of Central Park. "It's spectacular."

"Yes, Samantha. It's quite lovely," Mona said while continuing to frown as she looked at her computer.

Her tone of voice worried me a bit, so I came back inside. "So... what's up?"

"More Maxine drama."

"What's the deal with this Maxine?"

Mona sighed. "Where do I begin?"

"Why don't you start at the beginning?" I suggested, sitting in the chair across from Mona and sucking down more of the miracle juice that is coffee. "How do you know Maxine? This is the first I've heard of her."

"We both came to New York City around the same time in the early '80s. Both right out of college. I arrived at Tina's not long before Maxine got her own place."

"You lived in that little room where I'm staying? Did your feet touch the wall when you slept?"

Mona laughed. "No, I had one of the rooms Tina rents out on the second floor. Maxine lived in the one next door. We only overlapped for a few weeks, but our paths continued to cross, and we stayed in touch."

"She worked at *Vogue* with you?"

"No, but our careers did bring us into contact. Maxine started at an advertising agency, then moved

Chapter Four

into public relations, ultimately launching her own firm representing clients in the luxury market—from five-star hotels and spas to skin care products and makeup to fashion. The same kinds of things I covered in the magazine."

"Fancy things."

Mona smiled and nodded. "Quite fancy. Maxine got the idea for this conference about 25 years ago after she helped curate items for some celebrity swag bags."

"Celebrity swag bags?"

"Gift bags filled with the sorts of the products Maxine represented, from smaller objects like fancy chocolates or fine wine to big-ticket items like jewelry or all-expense paid trips to luxury resorts, offered to nominees and presenters at award shows—movie stars, in other words."

"Aren't movie stars already kind of set for those things?" I said, realizing what a rube I sounded like as it came out of my mouth.

"They are. And half the time they just give the products to their assistants, but from a marketing standpoint, the fact that you can say a celebrity used your product or stayed in your hotel held immense power. And this was before the whole influencer craze. They cracked down on swag bags at some of the award shows when the IRS started taxing the contents, but the idea set a precedent. Maxine immediately recognized the marketing potential of getting her clients' products into the hands of high-profile people. And, equally important, letting high-profile people know about the latest trends or travel hotspots. Maxine started a weekly newsletter highlighting her latest and greatest finds. People paid a lot of money to both receive that list and be mentioned on it. For a time, it was the ultimate insider's guide."

"Win-win."

Mona nodded. "Maxine then created the Business of Luxury conference as a way to bring her list to life. Similar to the newsletter, Maxine curates the list of attendees—buyers, suppliers, speakers—bringing the top players in the luxury products market together for three days of hobnobbing."

"Hobnobbing, eh?"

Mona smiled. "Yes, hobnobbing, Samantha. Each year, Maxine books a high-end hotel in the city that is either new or wants to show off a renovation and talks them into offering the rooms and meeting space for free with the conference just paying for the food and beverage costs. She spins it as a marketing coup for the hotel."

"Sounds like marketing makes the world go 'round," I said.

Mona touched her index finger to her nose and nodded. "Maxine also brings the New York tourism folks in as one of the sponsors. They offer the meeting planner and travel agent attendees tickets to the latest art exhibits or Broadway shows or tours through Central Park or along the High Line to entice them to bring their clients to the city."

"More marketing."

"Exactly."

"Pretty smart."

"Maxine is nothing if not savvy, but as Winston mentioned, she also has her demons."

✦ Chapter Four ✦

"You mentioned rehab."

"The woman likes her high-end vodka—and other mind-altering chemicals—a little too much."

"That's sad."

"It's very sad. When we first moved to the city in the '80s, we were young and the city was rather wild. I mean, we all hit the town. A lot. Late-night outings that involved a lot of cosmopolitans... or more illicit substances."

"Mona!"

"Sorry if this is too salacious for you, Sam."

I smiled. "I'm just teasing. Go on."

"For most of us, that was as far as it went, but Maxine, even then, had a tendency to overdo. You name it, she tried it. In those days, it was cocaine, then ecstasy. More recently, she's touted ketamine infusions and ayahuasca retreats."

"Wow."

"Right? I mean, that's kind of how she's lived her life in general: over the top in every way possible and always looking for the next greatest thing, which often means the latest, greatest high. You'll see when you meet her. I suppose it's part of why she's so successful. It also means she's stepped on a lot of people's toes and occasionally needs to take a break at the 'spa in the Hamptons' when it all comes crashing down."

Mona paused and looked outside at the view of what looked like it was going to be a gorgeous spring day. "As you know, I love this city. It's big and loud and brash and fabulous." She got a wistful smile on her face as a few car horns and sirens accentuated her description. "I miss living here in a lot of ways, but I also appreciate the quieter pleasures found in a place like Carmel."

And the time you spend with Uncle Henry, I thought.

"People like Maxine thrive on the chaos," Mona continued. "In their own way, so does the crowd at Tina's—and Tina herself. But while Tina flourishes in a way that's creative and inclusive and fun, Maxine, well… That intensity kind of does a number on her. You'll see." Mona sighed. "As soon as we find her."

"What is it exactly you'd like me to do to help, Mona?"

"I'm not sure. But you do have an eagle eye, my dear, so I'm thinking that maybe you'll find something we missed."

"I guess the first question is when did you—or anybody—last see her?"

"Maxine was here two days ago for the final pre-conference site visit with the hotel representatives. She left her suitcase, said she had an errand to run, and walked out of the hotel as her team was setting up the show office. She hasn't been seen or heard from since."

"She didn't go home?"

"We checked with the doorman at her building, but he hadn't seen her. The super conducted a wellness check, and her apartment was empty. And none of the staff has seen her here at the hotel. They have a room for her in the penthouse—it's going to be used as the hospitality suite…"

"Hospitality suite?"

"A place where attendees can do business or relax. I think Harriet mentioned some of the vendors would

Chapter Four

be offering mini spa sessions there as a way to market their products."

There was the M-word again.

"It would be like this suite but larger," Mona continued. "You know, an indoor-outdoor space filled with drinks and snacks plus stations set up for mini-facials, hair blow-outs, and foot massages."

"Oh my."

"But then Maxine never came back to the Penthouse Suite before the conference setup, which is scheduled for tomorrow."

"How do you know she didn't go to the suite?"

"The key card. They handed Maxine the packet with her room key card while they were on the site visit. According to the front desk, the door hasn't been activated."

"Hmmm."

We both pondered for a moment.

"How about this?" Mona said. "Why don't I start by showing you around the hotel and the people and places involved in the conference, and you can let me know what you think?"

"That works."

CHAPTER FIVE

Mona closed the door to her suite, and we headed back down the hall, where Leonora was somehow already waiting. I noticed that on this floor, there was only one elevator while there were three on the lobby level, so I asked about that.

"Those other elevators go to the floors with public spaces," Leonora said. "The Françoise has always had an attendant for the guest room floors."

"See, Sam, you are already noticing things I hadn't," Mona whispered to me before asking Leonora to take us to the show office.

Leonora pushed the button for the basement level. There, we found a series of halls leading to smaller meeting rooms. I noted that this floor of The Françoise was different from the lobby and the suite where Mona was staying—more utilitarian, and since it was underground, lacking any windows to the outside

Chapter Five

world. Still well-appointed, just not as snazzy. And quiet. It was really, really quiet. We reached a room with a small card on the door displaying the Business of Luxury logo, a.k.a. the "show office."

When Mona opened the door, the noise level took a big jump. Inside, we found about a dozen people peering into computers or talking on phones. I was able to make out a few snippets from the conversations.

"Just confirming that setup begins at 9 a.m. tomorrow in the Gold Room."

"Yes, your tabletop includes a power strip."

"Make sure the videographer gets shots of all the signage during setup."

The hub of activity was mesmerizing. At the sound of the door opening, they all looked up at Mona and me standing in the doorway. I had a weird déjà vu back to the moment I interrupted the dinner party the night before. Between the jet lag and sleeping in a closet—and the noise of the city, let's not forget the noise (except, it appeared, here on the basement level of The Françoise)—my mind was all askew. But this time, instead of Tiny Tina greeting me with a hug, most of them offered a rattled nod or a small wave and got back to the business at hand. I noticed they were all quite young. All, that is, except a woman in the back, who with her gray hair, looked to be around Mona's age, if not nearly as stylish. She gestured for us to wait until she got off her phone call.

"As you can see, this is the show office," Mona whispered.

Never having worked at a conference, the "show office" concept was new to me, but as I thought about it, not unexpected. An event would need an organizational hub, right?

"I see that," I whispered back. "Everyone looks quite young."

"Maxine uses interns. She calls them ambassadors—her 'luxury ambassadors.' Doesn't have to pay them much. You know, it's 'for the experience.'" Back to the air quotes.

I noticed more annoyance seeping into Mona's voice every time she talked about Maxine. As if on cue, the woman in the back sighed, loud enough I could hear it across the room, before saying, "Still no word? You're sure?" Another sigh. "Okay, thank you for your help."

The woman handed the phone to a young man with short red hair and horn-rimmed glasses standing next to her before making her way toward us. I may have undersold things when I said she wasn't nearly as stylish at Mona. Quite unlike every other person I had come into contact with so far, her clothes were about as plain as possible: utilitarian-looking beige pants and a gray crew-neck sweater. It was almost as if she was trying to disappear into her bland clothes while the gray hair she had pulled into a thick braid radiated an earth-mother quality. Neither was something I had seen in New York in my admittedly short time in the city.

"Mona, I'm so glad to see you," she said, giving her a warm hug, before turning to me. "You must be Samantha. I'm Harriet."

"It's so nice to meet you," I said, shaking her hand. "I'm so sorry for what you've been going through."

Chapter Five

Harriet rolled her eyes and gave a rueful smile. "I would say it's somewhat de rigueur when working with Maxine Martinique, but she's really done it this time. And the conference starts tomorrow. Our conference."

Tears formed in her eyes. I felt for the woman. From what Tina and her friends had told me last night, Harriet had as much invested in this conference as Maxine.

"Sam is here to help," said Mona. "I am going to show her the conference rooms and then maybe head up to Maxine's room here at the hotel…"

"…even if she never checked into it," Harriet finished.

"Yes," Mona said. "It's all I can think to do at this point."

"Have you called the police?" I asked both of them.

"Of course," Harriet said. "Since Maxine has been known to just take off from time to time, they wrote it off as a voluntary disappearance. Scarlet used her connections and got some officers to track her phone, which had been turned off, and perform a wellness check with her building superintendent, but the apartment was empty. They told us to call all the area hospitals and rehab centers, which we did. They said that's pretty much all we can do at this point."

I thought about the conference of cops Roger was attending across town and wondered if any of them could help, but just repeated "I'm sorry." It was all I could think of to say.

"A walk through the hotel sounds like a good idea," said Harriet. "That's the last place we all saw her before she walked out the door, turned off her phone, and seemingly disappeared into thin air. Let me know if you find anything. We'll just keep moving forward as if the conference is beginning as usual tomorrow night with the opening reception in the Gold Room."

Mona gave Harriet a reassuring pat on the arm, and we made our way up to the lobby level via one of the elevators without an attendant. I noticed the numbers in those elevators didn't go above the third floor. Back on the lobby level, we turned left and passed a couple of upscale-looking shops before stopping in the doorway of a large room featuring rows of chairs lined up facing a stage. Portraits of classic stage actors graced the walls.

"This is the Barrymore Room, where the education sessions will be held," Mona said.

I nodded as I looked around the room. "It is a gorgeous hotel."

Mona smiled. "Indeed, it is. It's always been one of my favorites."

"In what way?"

"I don't know. The history, the elegance. It's one of the grand New York hotels built in the early 1900s, along with hotels like The Pierre, The Plaza, The Carlyle, and the Waldorf-Astoria. Each of them has something special, but this one... I don't know. It exudes a certain warmth in addition to its old-world elegance, if that makes sense." She thought for a moment. "As I recall, the hotel was originally named for the owner's daughter, and they all lived in the building next door, which was designed as the family's mansion. The owner almost lost The Françoise

Chapter Five

after the stock market crash in 1929 but was able to sell off the mansion to keep the hotel going."

"Interesting," I said. I loved learning the stories of these old hotels. Reminded me of the history of the Lake Tahoe Lodge, which I had just written about for the magazine. The big difference was that while the lodge had gone through a crazy series of additions and renovations over the years, this one had seemingly retained its original Gilded Age glamour.

Mona got a wistful look on her face. "I still remember the first interview I conducted here when I started at *Vogue*. I was following a hot young stylist as she prepped models for the Met Gala."

"Fancy. Did the hotel look a lot different then?"

"Not really, thank goodness." Mona smiled. "It's always been so special. Like a lot of old hotels, it went through a period where it was starting to show its age, but they did a wonderful job updating everything without losing its charm."

We next stopped at the Gold Room, a larger ballroom with high ceilings and, as its name suggested, gold leaf appliqués and a large gold-and-crystal chandelier. You could almost picture the formal balls that must've taken place within these walls a century earlier.

"The opening reception, meals, and exhibitor marketplace will be held here," Mona said.

"It's a stunning room."

"Yes. An ideal venue for the conference." Mona sighed. "Assuming we can find Maxine in time."

We then returned to the front part of the lobby and walked over to the lounge I noticed when I first arrived. Although there was still a rope across the entrance indicating it was closed, I could see a long bar across the back wall and a cabaret-style space with a grand piano in the corner.

"More informal networking will take place here in the lobby lounge," Mona said.

More networking? I thought. Then I noticed what looked to be another elevator, tucked in the corner opposite that of the cabaret setup with a "closed" sign on it.

"Where does that go?" I asked.

"That elevator takes people to the hotel's rooftop bar."

"Rooftop bar? Fun!"

"Yes. It's new. They're everywhere these days. Much more popular than when I lived in the city. I believe it opens at 5 p.m."

Adding all these venues to Maxine's "hospitality" suite, I started to get the picture that networking was the real focus of the whole endeavor. I mean, yes, duh, bringing people together is the focus of any in-person gathering. I just hadn't thought it through, being a neophyte to the whole thing.

As we continued peering into the lounge from the lobby, a tall, older, seriously handsome man came up behind Mona. At six feet tall, Mona was taller than most (even Henry just came eye to eye with her), but this man beat her by a few inches. He was dressed in an impeccably tailored suit that reminded me of something James Bond might wear. Actually, he kind of looked like a retired James Bond.

Chapter Five

"Mona Reynolds," the man said, in a deep voice with what sounded like a generically continental accent, "I heard you were gracing our hotel this week."

I could see Mona make a slight start at the man's voice. She turned her head. "Georg," she said, pronouncing it "Gayorg" like Captain Von Trapp in *The Sound of Music*. (See what I mean by continental? And, yes, Georg Von Trapp became his nickname.) "So nice to see you."

"And you," Georg said, taking Mona's hand in his and holding it just a bit longer than one normally does.

I could again detect a moment of, I'm not sure what, but Mona was definitely a little agitated. "I somehow missed the announcement that you were the general manager here."

That was suspicious. The Mona I knew missed nothing.

"Not the general manager. I'm the vice president of new development for Hotels du Jour," Georg said. "I've been overseeing The Françoise since the acquisition. Naturally, with the recent renovation and our hosting the Business of Luxury, I thought it appropriate that I be on site for the event." He gestured to the compact, yet incredibly shiny, suitcase he carried behind him. "I just flew in from Gstaad."

The sexy tone he used when he said, "I just flew in from Gstaad" even turned me on a little. I could see it totally rattled Mona. I wasn't sure of their history, but you could cut the sexual tension with a knife. And they were both, you know, in their 60s. Like old. Kind of gross. I mean, here I was just getting used to the idea of Mona and Henry hanging out. Then I learned about her bawdy, drug-filled younger days in New York. And now someone I was almost positive she'd had some sort of hot love affair with was unabashedly flirting with her.

"I'm so pleased to hear about your new position," Mona said with a very measured voice. "Most well deserved."

"I heard you left New York," Georg said, raising his eyebrows along with the pheromone levels in the room.

"Yes," Mona said. "A few years ago, to take over the editor-in-chief position at *Carmel Today* magazine."

"Well, the city is much less bright without you in it," he said. Even my knees buckled. I couldn't wait to hear from Mona what the heck the story was with this guy.

"You flatter me," Mona said, regaining her composure and adding a touch of flirting to her voice as well. By this point, I wondered if I should pretend to need the bathroom to give them space. Except that I felt proprietary toward Uncle Henry and was afraid they'd run off to a desert island if I left them alone. Then she surprised the hell out of me by saying, "And how's your lovely wife, Desiree?"

What? Wife? The man who was practically humping Mona (figuratively and in the most elegant way possible, of course) had a wife? And the way Mona hit the word "Desiree," you could tell she was not particularly fond of the woman.

"She's doing well," Georg said in a rather subdued tone that was somewhat unreadable. "I will pass along your regards."

★ Chapter Five ★

I wasn't quite sure what I was supposed to do or say. Luckily, at that moment, Mona—perhaps sensing my predicament—looked at me and said, "I'm so sorry, Georg. Where are my manners? Let me introduce Samantha Powers, our travel columnist at *Carmel Today*. Samantha, Georg Keller."

"Travel columnist?" Georg said, turning to look at me. "Sounds like someone I should get to know. So nice to meet you, Samantha Powers."

"You can call me Sam," I managed to eke out as he shook my hand. I noted his nails were impeccably groomed. Better than mine, if I was being honest.

"Georg has managed some of the top five-star hotels all over the world," Mona said. "Including those owned by his wife's family's company, Hotels du Jour."

Oooo. That was an interesting little tidbit.

"I live to serve," he said, ignoring the last comment and turning back to look directly at Mona, making both of our knees buckle a little bit. Dammit, man. "Speaking of which, how can I help you today?"

"Well, we're trying to figure out what happened to Maxine."

"Maxine?" An almost imperceptible dark shadow went across his face at her name. "I'm sorry, I don't understand. Her conference starts tomorrow. Did something happen to her? The staff informed me that she was at the pre-con two days ago."

"And she hasn't been seen since," Mona said.

"Oh, I had no idea. As I said, I just flew in from our hotel in Gstaad," Georg said. *Dammit man, stop saying that!* "I was told she had booked the Penthouse Suite for the totality of the conference, and these preparatory days, of course."

Now I could see at least one of the reasons for the shadow. Maxine was taking what sounded like the most expensive room in the hotel for almost a full week—and from what Mona told me earlier, on a complimentary basis.

"I don't have any information on this hotel yet, so let me check with the front desk as to the status of the suite," Georg continued.

When Georg left to walk—it was more of an executive saunter—over to the front desk, I turned back to Mona and whispered, "You have some explaining to do, missie."

"I have no idea what you mean, Samantha," Mona said, but the blush in her cheeks betrayed her.

Before I could prod further, Georg returned (sans his shiny suitcase). "The front desk informed me that the room has been booked for Ms. Martinique, but nobody has seen her and the electronic sensor in the front door was never activated." He held up a key card. "They've given me a master key, so why don't we all go check it out?"

We trooped back to the elevator, where Georg greeted Leonora warmly and asked about her family members—by name—just as he had with three other employees we passed in the lobby. I could see he had an incredible touch with people, which is probably why he'd lasted as long as he had in the hospitality industry.

When the wand on the bronze plaque above the door reached the PH on the far right, Leonora opened

Chapter Five

the gates. We each thanked Leonora and walked down to a large double doorway emblazoned with the words "Penthouse Suite." I noted a single door farther down the hall. I thought it might be the stairway, but then I noticed that there was another door with an exit sign at the opposite end of the hall.

Before I could ask where the door led, Georg said, "That's odd." I turned to see him staring at the area to the right of the double doors leading to the suite.

"What?" Mona asked.

Georg pointed to a small panel on the right of the doorway, where an almost imperceptible red light was lit. "The 'do not disturb' is illuminated. You can only do that from inside the suite."

He knocked and called out "Management!" a few times before using the key card to open the door. As we entered, my first impression was, well, *wow!* I thought Mona's suite was large. The Penthouse Suite was immense. I could see why it would be used for hospitality. You could easily fit a few dozen people in the living area, which included what looked to be a fully stocked bar and a working kitchen. As Harriet and the hotel staff had predicted, it was perfectly pristine, as if no one had been there. Beyond the living area, the terrace was also larger than the one in Mona's suite and, because it was at the far end of the building, offered a perfect view of Central Park. When Mona went outside to check it out, I noticed a set of closed double doors to the right.

"Is that the bedroom?" I asked.

"The primary, yes."

"Primary?"

Georg smiled. "We don't call them masters anymore. But it is the main living quarters for this suite. A second bedroom can be found on the other side of the kitchen and has its own entrance." Ah, the other door in the hall made sense now. "We leave both closed off when the rest of the space is to be used as a hospitality suite," Georg continued.

I nodded at the door to the primary bedroom. "Do you mind if I take a look?"

"The travel columnist for *Carmel Today*?" he said with a smile. "I'd be honored and hope you will mention it—and the rest of the hotel—in your story."

I didn't mention that Mona was writing the story and instead smiled and opened the door. Well, I tried, and found it was locked.

"Oh, sorry about that," Georg said. "As I mentioned, we keep the bedroom doors closed and locked to ensure the privacy of the guests staying in the suite."

Georg stepped up to use the key card, again knocking and calling out "Management!" as he opened the door.

As I stepped inside, I was surprised to see that, unlike the living area, the bedroom looked as if it had been slept in and a suitcase lay open beside it. "I thought you said that Maxine never accessed her room," I said.

"That's what the front desk told me," Georg said with a frown. "They gave her the packet with her key cards at the pre-con walk-through and had her bag delivered to her room. I was told she then left the hotel and hasn't been back since."

* Chapter Five *

With Top Hat Renaldo safeguarding the door and Levitating Leonora at the elevator, it did seem kind of impossible to sneak back into this hotel. On the other hand, someone had slept in that bed.

"Hello? Management!" Georg called out again as we continued into the bedroom. He pushed open the glass doors to the left of the bed to reveal a private patio bordered by a tall black gate. Nothing there. He then walked back around the bed toward the closed door to the bathroom.

"Maxine, are you in there?" Georg called, knocking. He pushed open the door. "Maxine? Oh my god!"

I followed him through the door and was startled to see a woman's body—I'm assuming that of the oft-mentioned Maxine—submerged in the large Jacuzzi-style tub. From my brief glimpse peering around Georg's arm, it appeared she had been dead for some time. A martini glass with two olives in it sat on the side of the tub next to an empty bottle of Laporte vodka and a vial with lettering on the side. I could just make out the letters "keta" as part of one of the words on the vial when Georg started pushing me back out of the bathroom, closed the door tightly, grabbed the house phone, and immediately asked for security.

Mona came walking into the bedroom. "What is going on?" she asked.

"It's Maxine. She's dead."

CHAPTER SIX

The gathering that night at Tina's brownstone was epic. Epic! A much bigger crowd than the one the night before filled the brownstone's living area. Once word got out about Maxine's untimely death, everybody seemed to know to make their way to Tina's for a wake of sorts. Spreadsheet Scarlet, Van Gogh Victor, and Sir Winston were there, of course, along with so many others. I met an amazing array of people: opera singers and actors and playwrights and professors and fashionistas and dancers (of course, there were dancers). There were also society types—old money, arts-supporting Upper East-Siders, Scarlet called them—who were both backers of Tina's dance academy and devotees of Maxine's newsletter.

All were buzzing about Maxine's death. I listened in to the conversations as well as I could.

Chapter Six

"Drowning in a hotel bathtub? It's so Whitney Houston of her."

"The poor dear won't get anywhere near the press she did, of course."

"If any. The Françoise has, of course, always been known for its discretion in deaths much more high profile than poor Maxine's."

"Discretion is their middle name."

"Since the days of Barrymore."

"It'll probably kill her—again—to be left off page 6."

"I don't think this is how she'll want to be remembered anyway."

"No doubt. No doubt."

There were hugs and sad, astonished, surprised, even somewhat resigned faces. I somehow ended up on door duty for those who didn't know the entry code. As soon as I would buzz them in, they'd take one look at me, realize they had no idea who I was, and move on to Tina. Of course, once Tina pointed me out as the one who discovered Maxine's body, I became more interesting. Then, when I said I didn't know anything, they'd again lose interest.

About that (discovering the body): After finding Maxine, Mona and I were quickly ushered down to an office behind the front desk that Georg used when he was in town. We were sequestered there while the hotel's security team and then NYPD officers examined "the scene." A uniformed police officer came to take our statements and then the medical examiner on duty came by to confirm the details of those statements. When we weren't being interviewed, Mona was calling everyone to give them the news. I sat close to the door, where I had a slight view of the lobby and could watch the activity out there. The lack of any body being wheeled through meant they had managed to get Maxine out through an entrance other than the one manned by Top Hat Renaldo. It made me wonder if that was how Maxine got up to her room in the first place. I mean, obviously the hotel had at least one service entrance, and it made sense they'd use it to take a dead body out. But why would Maxine use it and not the main entrance to go to her room? And what about the door mechanism not being breached, but the do-not-disturb being lit from inside the suite? It was all so odd.

After the medical examiner confirmed our statements and our contact information, we were told we could go. Mona and I went down to the show office in the basement and met with the members of the Business of Luxury team, who had also been interviewed. Harriet wasn't there. It was just the young "ambassadors," who didn't seem all that crushed to learn Maxine was gone. From what I could gather from their chattering, Harriet really ran everything. Maxine's death just meant they wouldn't be distracted from the task at hand by her visits. If anything, it sounded like Maxine just made things more difficult—making last-minute requests that were impossible or berating them for not reading her mind when she wanted something.

Since there wasn't much I could do and Mona wanted to wait for Harriet, I suggested that I head back to Tina's. Mona nodded and said she would meet me there. I left The Françoise, but instead of going straight

Chapter Six

back, I decided to take a detour toward Central Park. I mean, I was in New York, so I should see some of the damn city, right? I found a bench to sit on at the edge of the park. I watched people walking down 5th Avenue seemingly without a care in the world. Well, they might have had cares, but not about the death of Maxine Martinique just a few feet and ten stories up from where they walked. I wondered what happened that day when Maxine left the hotel, only to disappear, and then reappear dead in her hotel room. What the hell happened in those 48 hours?

I pulled out my phone and decided to call Roger, even though I was still disappointed in what felt like a blow-off earlier. I got his voicemail: "This is Detective Roger Kai. Please leave a message, and I will call you back." Always so formal, but I did like hearing his voice.

"Hey, Roger," I said, after the beep. "I know you're busy, but I just wanted to say I hope you are having a better day than I am. We found the gal who disappeared, and she's, well, I guess there's no way to say this except that she's dead. Drowned in the bathtub, it would seem. The medical examiner says natural causes. Who knows? Hey, maybe some of your new forensics friends could weigh in." I laughed to let him know it was a joke. Kind of. "Anyway, I'm headed back to Tina's, but thought I'd see if there was a chance you might want to grab something to eat in the Midtown area. I think that's kind of close to where you are, and I just realized I haven't eaten all day."

I clicked "end call" and started walking down 5th Avenue, occasionally pulling out my phone to make sure I hadn't missed a message. Nope. I passed fancy hotels that looked similar to The Françoise—Pierre, Sherry Netherland, Plaza—and a huge subterranean Apple store. I then spotted a tiny sign that said "Aldo's Pizza" on a side street and found a pizzeria sandwiched between a juice shop and a bodega on the ground floor of a large building. After hearing multiple people extol the virtues of New York-style pizza, I decided to check it out. I ordered a pepperoni slice and a soda and found a seat at the counter.

I had to admit the pizza was pretty darn yummy and not just because I was starving. While I ate, I watched more of the bustling activity of the city outside. I was kind of starting to love it. So many people going in so many directions. So many stories! I even thought I might have seen Tina's nephew Hastings walking quickly across the street. Yelling at him from a block away seemed fruitless, so I continued enjoying my pizza in silence (the silence being relative, of course).

I finally felt the vibration that meant a text had come in. I pulled out my phone to see that it was from Roger. "Sorry about your friend. Still super busy. Talk later."

Really? That's it? Not even a smiling face with heart eyes emoji? I finished my pizza and walked the rest of the way back to Tina's a little more dejected. When I reached the brownstone, I used the keypad code Tina had given me to unlock the door and made my way into the living area. Similar to the first time I arrived at the brownstone, I was immediately enfolded into a hug by Tiny Tina.

Chapter Six

"Oh, Sam. Oh, Sam!" Tina said. "How horrible that you found her."

"I'm so sorry for your loss," I said, using the words I heard innumerable times after the death of my mother a decade earlier.

Tears fell from her eyes. "We always worried that the drinking would do her in."

I wasn't sure if I should mention the odd circumstances or the small vial I noticed sitting alongside the vodka bottle, so I didn't.

"I'm so sorry," I repeated.

"I know you are," Tina said, tears falling from her eyes. "I do my best to protect these girls who arrive on my doorstep. Even those who arrived more than 40 years ago."

Tina offered a wry smile and suddenly looked every inch of her at least 80 (if I had to guess) years. Then, just as quickly, she snapped out of it.

"I hope you don't mind helping me out, Samantha," Tina said. "We're having an impromptu gathering for Maxine, and people will start arriving soon."

No sooner were the words out of her mouth than the door started buzzing—or just clicking open for those who knew the code. They came bearing food and wine and stories, lots of stories. Most seemed to be about Maxine's wild antics. I was kind of sorry I'd never had a chance to meet the woman. She definitely sounded like a character. Bigger than life, but with a temper you didn't want to cross and a propensity to occasionally go off the deep end. Pretty much the opposite of both Mona, with her sophisticated grace, and Tina, with her loving spirit.

Most of the people were at least Mona's age, but there were a few closer to my age or even younger. I found myself gravitating toward a group of the younger crew hanging out in the kitchen—actors, musicians, and grad students who'd spent time in the house. If I had to sum up their vibe, it would be "driven." Listening to their stories, I felt kind of lazy and undirected. What was worrying about leaks or a sticking front door compared to producing your own one-woman show in a one-act festival or writing an art history dissertation? Luckily, my job as a travel writer gave me a touch of cachet, even if it was only a part-time gig.

Hastings arrived later in the evening. He nodded to me from outside the kitchen doorway, and I headed out to meet him. I noted again just how good-looking the boy was. Purely aesthetically speaking, of course.

"So… your first full day in the city…" Hastings said, as we stood to the side of the entrance to the kitchen. I could see the gathering in the living area had grown even larger.

"A little dramatic," I said.

"Just a little," he said, laughing. "Sorry to laugh, but that had to be crazy. Finding her like that."

"Definitely. How well did you know Maxine?" I asked him.

He thought for a moment. "She was around my whole life, so I guess pretty well." He paused again. "Although I'm not sure all that many people really knew her."

What an odd thing to say. "I'm not sure what you mean by that."

Chapter Six

"Well, Maxine liked to grace us with her presence in a very flamboyant way. Very Auntie Mame, if you know the play." I didn't but got the gist. "She would swing by Aunt Tina's dinners or come by to bestow us with products from a new client or regale us with the story of her latest adventure at a lavish hotel in the Maldives or on a luxury yacht off Sardinia. That kind of stuff. And then she'd be off. To me, it always felt like an act and that she never wanted anyone to see too much, if that makes sense." He smiled and thought for another moment. "When I was a kid, she terrified me."

"Terrified you? How so?"

"I don't know. Her energy. It was so... I don't know. Oversized? It was a lot. I lived in fear of having it turned on me if I did something wrong. Saw it happen more than once—" He laughed. "Like when someone called her 'Max' or 'Maxie' instead of using her full name."

As someone who preferred people call her "Sam" instead of Samantha, I found that kind of funny.

"She did not like that," he emphasized, "especially after she took that French husband's last name: Martinique. According to Aunt Tina, the persona of Maxine Martinique—complete with the pseudo-European accent—was quite different from the Maxie Saunders who moved to New York from Petaluma. Volatile temper included."

I shuddered. I very much understood the fear engendered when dealing with someone who had that kind of temper. It was how I felt around my ex-boyfriend, a.k.a. he who shall not be named. We had worked together when I was at the newspaper in Los Angeles—me a crime reporter on the Metro section and him an editor at the Sports copy desk. He was one of those people everybody loved. Super clever. Bigger than life. But after we got together, I grew to fear the times that bigger-than-life energy would turn on me. The first time it happened, I left him. He apologized and pulled me back in. It became a cycle that happened nine times in the three years we were together. It left me seriously unbalanced and out of control. The cycle continued until I moved back to Carmel to take care of my dad and ended things for good. I had to admit it was one of the reasons I appreciated how even-keeled Roger was. Not that his calm demeanor eliminated the occasional unbalanced feeling, I realized, as I looked at my phone. Still no message after the "talk later." Sigh.

Hastings glanced over at Tiny Tina bouncing between groups of people. "I mean, I know Maxine loved Aunt Tina, the way everyone does." He smiled.

I smiled as well. "Tina is pretty amazing. Do your parents live close by?"

"Oh no," Hastings said. "My parents died in a car crash when I was a baby. I grew up here with Tina."

"Oh, I am so sorry," I said and felt another small shiver as my mom had also died in a car crash. *Geez, dude, you certainly are inadvertently pushing a lot of my buttons.*

"Thanks," Hasting said with a wry smile. "Truth be told, I don't remember them at all. Tina and Horatio raised me as their own child. And only child. They never had any of their own. Of course, there were

Chapter Six

always tons of other kids around, especially in the afternoons and during the summers when Tina ran her dance camps. And I was surrounded by Aunt Tina's friends, like Mona before she moved, and Winston and Scarlet and Victor... and Harriet and Dmitri, of course."

"Dmitri?"

"Harriet's son. You didn't meet him? He started helping out with the conference after he got out of the military."

As he said that, we both turned to see Mona enter the living area, followed by Harriet, who had obviously been crying, and who I now learned was her son, Dmitri. I recognized him as the young man with the red hair and glasses that Harriet handed her phone to when I first met her in the show office. Huh. On closer inspection, he did appear to be a few years older than the other "ambassadors." Like Harriet, he seemed to do his best to try to fade into the background. Hastings nodded in his direction.

"Oh, I saw him over at The Françoise but didn't get to meet him," I said. "You grew up with him?"

"Yeah, when Harriet started working with Maxine, he would follow her wherever she went or Harriet would drop him off here for Tina to babysit—which usually meant me looking after him. I was maybe ten, but you kind of grow up fast in this city."

"I can see that," I said, laughing.

"I think his dad was in the military, too. Desert Storm or something? I never met him."

I looked back at the two of them. As Harriet entered the room, everyone moved to envelop her in a hug. That was sweet. When Mona saw me, she nodded and started walking in my direction.

"Do you mind?" I asked Hastings, gesturing to Mona.

"Not at all," he said. He continued into the kitchen as I walked over to meet her.

"So… What's going on?" I asked.

"Well," Mona said, pulling me to the side, "the medical examiner is ruling it an accidental death. She said it appears Maxine just fell asleep in the bath—perhaps aided by more than a few martinis—and drowned. She'd been dead for some time."

"And the conference?"

"Harriet and Dmitri and the rest of their team consulted with the sponsors and attendees, and everyone thinks we should go ahead with it."

"Wow."

"Yes, wow. They're spinning it as a tribute to Maxine. I personally would have preferred to cancel. I would think their liability insurance would cover the costs." Mona sighed. "Instead, I will be on stage tomorrow talking about trends in the luxury market as if nothing has happened."

Mona's voice cracked. I had never seen her so stressed and wondered what was really going on in there.

"I'm so sorry" was all I could think to say. Again.

"I know you are, dear."

"So, I guess that means I'll be going home?"

Mona's eyes got wide. "Oh, I hope you won't, Samantha."

Chapter Six

"Really? I mean, you asked me here to help find Maxine and I, well, we did."

"Yes, but I could use your support. As could Tina." She paused. "I'm going to be honest. Something doesn't feel right about Maxine's death."

"It does seem a bit wonky that she was in her room at the hotel the whole time without anybody knowing."

"Yes, right? I wouldn't use the word 'wonky' but yes. I don't know. Something doesn't feel right. After you left, I tried to talk to the NYPD detective in charge." She pulled a card out of her pocket and looked at it. "Detective Garcia. He could not have been more bored by the whole thing. They will run some tests, but it's not a high priority as the medical examiner's preliminary ruling was drowning-induced cardiac arrest. Essentially, she fell asleep and didn't wake up when the water engulfed her. Either way, Detective Garcia said it was obviously an accidental death, and he would be filing his report saying as much."

"Did you see the actual report? Or the chrono?"

Maxine stopped a bit at the word "chrono" and then smiled. "I sometimes forget your father was the police chief."

"And Uncle Henry teaches criminal law, and I covered crime at the newspaper…"

Mona got a small smile on her face at the mention of Henry's name. "True. And no, they showed us nothing. When Harriet asked for a copy of the report, Detective Garcia said we had to request it in writing."

"And what about Maxine's, I don't know, stuff? Estate?"

"That will be a whole other kettle of fish that luckily has nothing to do with us. I'm assuming the company and Business of Luxury conference was co-owned with Harriet, so she'll get that. There's Maxine's co-op and who knows what else she has socked away. The woman was married four times, but not currently, and she didn't have children with any of them. She has no family that I've ever heard of—beyond the family she has here with Tina…" That was odd, although I suppose they considered themselves family. "Who knows where it will all go?"

Just then, Georg entered the living area, I'm sure to pay his respects as well. Still impeccably dressed, he gave his usual charming smile and walked up to Tina to give her a hug.

"Tina, it's been too long," he said. "I'm so sorry we have to come together under such sad circumstances."

I couldn't be sure, but based on the body language, Tina did not like this man AT ALL. Odd because, in the short time since I'd met her, Tina seemed to love everybody. That and Georg's superpower seemed to be the ability to make everybody love him.

Oh my, what a kettle of fish (to use Mona's expression) we seemed to have gotten ourselves into, which is why I surprised even myself with the words I heard coming from my mouth.

"Okay, I'll stay. As long as you need."

CHAPTER SEVEN

Famous last words, huh? I woke up the next morning in my closet at Tina's, sweater again tied around my eyes and ears to help me sleep, wondering how the hell the day was going to play out. I knew I would be heading back to the hotel to help Mona in any way I could and to try to alleviate the wonkiness we both felt about Maxine's death. It just bugged me not knowing how and why Maxine snuck into the hotel with no one able to see her. I mean, from all accounts, the woman had not treated her health all that well, to say the least, considering all the rehab visits, so passing out or suffering a heart attack and sinking into the tub was not out of the realm of possibilities. But why turn off her phone, sneak into her hotel room, and turn on the "do not disturb"? What was that all about?

The best place to find the answer lay with the staff of The Françoise, a.k.a. my new friends Top Hat Renaldo and Levitating Leonora, and the Business of Luxury conference team—Harriet, Dmitri, and all those young ambassadors. Luckily, I had a perfect excuse to talk to everybody as Mona decided that with me staying in New York and her helping Harriet out with the conference, I should go ahead and plan to write the Splendid Adventures story as usual. I could cover the renovations at The Françoise and hit the sights of the city scheduled for the attendees by the tourism bureau. I wasn't sure if that meant I'd get to move over to the hotel, but the thought buoyed me as I used the phone booth-sized bathroom to take a shower and the postcard-sized mirror to attempt to make myself semi-presentable—and pretended I didn't see any small furry creatures moving in the alley behind the building. I again packed up my bag just in case, snuck through the kitchen and past the happy dancers in the front room, and headed out to The Françoise.

As I walked to the bus, I started reveling in the sounds of the city and noticed my pace picking up to match the New Yorkers. I even passed a lady pushing a stroller with a dog trailing behind. Slackers! *Aha! Look at me, continuing my transformation into a New Yorker*, I thought, giving a wave and a smile to the dog. (Again, I am not a monster.) I passed the sculptures in the median on Park Avenue and made my way to the bus stop in front of the Morgan Library on Madison. As I waited, I felt a buzz that meant a text had come in.

Roger.

* Chapter Seven *

"Sorry I've been MIA," it read. "I have a break this afternoon. Want to meet halfway? Maybe a walk in Central Park? I could use an escape from this hotel."

"I would like that," I texted back, adding a smile emoji to match the smile on my face. My day was already looking up.

When I walked into The Françoise, I found a rush of activity in the lobby. People were checking in at the hotel's front desk and then again at a long table that had been set up against the far wall, where I spotted the now black-clad Business of Luxury ambassadors handing out nametags on lanyards. Other people were carting large bins in the direction of the Gold Room, where Mona told me the vendors would be exhibiting their products. A large banner hung prominently in the lobby proclaiming, "Welcome to the Business of Luxury."

"Good morning, Ms. Powers. So good to see you again," a familiar voice said before I could even spot the top hat.

"Good morning, Renaldo. How are you this morning?"

"I am quite well. Thank you for asking. Are you here to see Ms. Reynolds?"

"I am."

"I believe I last saw her heading into our vice president's office."

"Thank you, Renaldo," I said, mentally figuring out how I was going to get the man alone to pick his brain. He obviously missed nothing. "May I?" I asked, pointing to the hallway behind the front desk that led to Georg's office, the same office where we had been sequestered the day before during the investigation into Maxine's death.

Renaldo nodded and I headed back. As I turned the corner that led to Georg's office, I could hear Mona and Georg talking in low voices that did not sound happy.

"...need to be told," Mona said.

"I don't agree, Mona," Georg said, in a tone not as cordial as before. "I'm not sure why you feel the need to bring up something that has, quite literally, died with Maxine."

"I..."

Before I could hear anything else, I spotted a woman wearing a well-tailored suit, heels (not legal in Carmel!), and hotel nametag coming out of an office at the far end of the hall. To keep anyone from discovering I was listening, I backed up and around the side of the front desk. I then again started walking toward Georg's office, calling out, "Mona?" as if I had just gotten there and couldn't remember which was his office.

"In here, Samantha," Mona said, in a tight voice.

I entered the office and found Georg sitting behind the desk, with Mona standing as far away as she could while still within the same room. She had her hands crossed over her chest and a most displeased look on her face that she attempted to adjust when I entered.

"I was just telling Georg that you will now be writing the story on the hotel and its renovations," Mona said in a bit of a fib. "He has graciously offered a room for you here at the hotel, should you decide you would rather stay here instead of at Tina's."

Chapter Seven

They both looked expectantly at me. "Well, I mean, if it would help with the story..." I said as demurely as possible while jumping up and down inside. I mean, I loved Tina and enjoyed the time I spent with Hunky Hastings, but that dark closet of a room kind of freaked me out.

"Perfect," Georg said, as the woman I'd seen at the end of the hall started walking past the door. "Oh, Candace?"

"Yes, Mr. Keller?" she said, stepping in the door. "Oh, hello, Ms. Reynolds." So formal, these hotel people in NYC!

Mona nodded. "Hello, Candace. This is Samantha Powers. Samantha is the travel columnist for *Carmel Today*."

"Such a beautiful magazine," Candace said. "I loved the story on the Mokihana Resort & Spa. I took my family there last year for our vacation. We had a wonderful time."

"I wrote that story," I said, beaming just a bit. (Sue me.)

"As you can see, Ms. Berkley keeps up with the travel press for the company," Georg said, the impeccable smile returning to his face. "That's why we are so happy you will be covering our hotel, especially after the renovations. Candace, do we have a room for Samantha?"

"Perhaps one near mine?" Mona asked.

"Of course," Candace said, pulling out a piece of paper from the clipboard she was carrying. "I was just going over the assigned rooms for the conference with Dmitri. I believe the room adjacent to your suite is available, Ms. Reynolds. If you wish, we could put Ms. Powers there. Unless, of course, she would prefer a suite of her own."

"A standard room is just fine," I said.

"Royal King, we call them," Candace said with a barely disguised smirk. I immediately got a playful vibe from her and gave her the nickname Candy Cane. With the jovial-yet-hip Mrs. Claus vibe she gave off, it fit.

"That sounds wonderful," Mona said. "Sam, why don't you go with Candace to get that set up, and I will see what Harriet needs for the conference?"

Mona gave me a somewhat rattled look and rushed out the door. That Georg sure knew how to push her buttons. I was definitely going to have to find out more about the two of them. I nodded to Georg and dutifully followed Candace out of the executive offices and around to the front desk. She spoke to the clerk for a few minutes and came back with a card key in a small envelope.

"Here you go," she said. "You're booked into room 736 under the same Business of Luxury account as Mona Reynolds. Should you and Ms. Reynolds both choose, you can open the door that adjoins the living area of Mona's suite. At the moment, it's closed and locked on both sides."

"Thank you, Candace. At some point, would you have time to give me a more thorough tour of the hotel?" I asked, thinking she was the type of person who might know where the bodies were buried (metaphorically speaking). "For the story, of course."

Chapter Seven

"Of course!" Candace said. "Today is a little crazy, with the conference move-in and all, but a group tour of the hotel is on the agenda after tonight's reception."

"Are you involved with the conference?"

"Yes, the Business of Luxury is my client," she said, beaming. "I'll be managing everything from the hotel side."

"So sad about Maxine," I said.

"So sad! I've worked with Ms. Martinique for years, of course."

"Here?"

"Here and other hotels." Candace laughed. "We move around a lot in this industry. Maxine was a client we all had to learn to…" She seemed to be looking for the right word. "Let's say, placate. Although things have changed since her 'To the Max' newsletter was first launched, it's still a coup to be mentioned. Same with their Instagram account. And, of course, booking the conference itself is the ultimate achievement."

"To the Max?" I asked. That was the first I'd heard the name of the newsletter. Kind of funny for a woman who hated for anyone to say her nickname in person to then use it as the name of her newsletter. Or maybe that was the reason she made the distinction. Without knowing the woman, it was hard to say.

"To the Max," Candace said, with another conspiratorial-type smirk. Oh yeah, she definitely knew where the bodies were buried and might be persuaded to blab a little. "I'm going to the ballroom now, if you'd like to see the setup for tonight's reception."

"I'd love that." I looked at the time on my phone. I had a couple of hours before I was scheduled to meet Roger.

We walked through the hotel lobby and then down the hall that would take us to the Gold Room.

"As you can see, Ms. Powers—" Candace started.

"Please, call me Sam," I said.

"Of course. Sam," she said with a smile. "As you can see, we are in the midst of setup for the exhibits."

I looked around the room, which was bustling with people opening boxes and travel cases and creating displays—some elaborate, some more simple—on tables that had been strategically placed close to the walls. Each table had small cards attached listing the name of the exhibitor. I also noted what looked to be a buffet and bar set up at the far end and high-top tables in the middle.

"The meals will be in here as well?"

"Tonight's reception will be here, as will the lunches as they coincide with the one-on-one meetings the attendees have with the exhibitors," Candace said with a smile.

"Makes sense." *All about the networking*, I thought.

Candace turned to look at someone struggling with a large case at the far end of the room. "I'm sorry. Can I help you with anything else?" she asked.

"No, please, go do what you need to do," I said. "I can check things out on my own. Thank you again for your help with the room. I'll see you at the reception tonight?"

"You can bet on it," she said with a warm smile.

Chapter Seven

Oh, I liked her. I started wandering among the exhibits, checking out the goodies people were offering. I saw spa products, makeup lines, and jewelry, including a line with diamond-studded dog and cat collars. There, I overheard a woman holding a Yorkie puppy modeling one of the collars saying, "Of course, Hamlet, Prince of Denmark has his own Instagram page. We just hit a half million followers." Blech.

As I passed another table, I overheard someone say, "I mean, really, what IS luxury…"

Hell if I know, lady, I thought as I came upon a table where a young woman with long straight black hair was struggling to push up the backing for a very tall poster featuring pictures of luxurious-looking travel options: safaris, tropical beaches, and ice hotels. At the top of the poster, a logo said: "Bespoke Adventures."

"Can I help you with that?" I offered.

"Oh, thank you," the woman said. "If you could grab the base, it makes it easier to push the rod that holds the poster up and clip it to the top."

"Got it," I said, holding the back of the base. "This is a pretty ingenious little contraption."

"It's a life-saver," she said, after clipping it into place. "I attend about 30 of these conferences a year, and it's so easy to fold back up and ship to the next site."

"That's a lot of conferences. All in New York?"

"No, mostly the US, though."

"No safaris or tropical resorts like in the photos, eh?" I said, pointing to the pictures.

"I wish. More like a Hilton in Des Moines or a Marriott in Houston. I attend a lot of regional meeting planner and travel agent conferences." She looked around at the Gold Room. "I have to say, this is one of the nicest. And they got us a great rate to stay here."

"Maxine did?"

"No, I don't even know Maxine. I deal with Harriet and Dmitri."

"Are you the owner of the company?" I said, pointing to the logo.

She laughed. "No, just their lowly rep." She turned to look more closely at me. "I'm so sorry. My name is Nikki Liu. I didn't get your name."

"Samantha—but you can call me Sam—Powers."

"Thanks, Sam. You work for the hotel?"

"Oh, no, I'm actually a travel writer for *Carmel Today* magazine."

"Then these are right up your alley," Nikki said, pointing to the gorgeous pictures on the poster.

"I guess," I said. "I'm still a little new at this."

"Do we have an appointment during tomorrow's marketplace?"

"No. I'm not here in any official capacity. My editor is speaking at the conference so I'm just helping out since, well, you know…"

"Oh, yeah, Maxine. Sad, right?" I have to say, she didn't seem that sad. "Again, I didn't really know her, beyond, well, this…"

Nikki looked down at her table and started flipping through the stacks of materials. She pulled a conference guide out from underneath her brochures and handed it to me. I started flipping through. It looked

Chapter Seven

a lot like a magazine filled with advertising from the companies I had just walked by. Instead of stories, it had pages listing the dates, times, and descriptions of the various sessions followed by small biographies of each of the sponsoring organizations and attendees. On the cover, underneath the "Business of Luxury" logo, was a picture taken on what I now recognized as the terrace outside the Penthouse Suite at The Françoise. A striking woman I assumed was Maxine (since I'd only gotten a glimpse of the woman in the bathtub) stood holding a martini in front of the beautifully landscaped railing with Central Park in the distance.

"Is this Maxine?"

Nikki looked. "Yeah. That's her." She laughed. "That's what all her conference guides look like. Last year, the Business of Luxury was held at the Algonquin, and she was photographed holding a martini in their newly renovated lobby lounge alongside their famous hotel cat, Hamlet."

"Do you mind if I take this?" I asked, gesturing to the guide.

"Of course not," she said, gesturing to the stack on her table, "they left plenty." She began pulling silver Bespoke Adventures-logoed suitcase tags out of boxes and placing them on the table. "Hey, thanks again for your help. Even if we don't have an official appointment, we should talk about getting you on one of our trips so you can write about it for the magazine."

"I would love that!"

"See you tonight at the reception?"

"Definitely," I said. "See you later."

As I walked out of the hotel, I looked more closely at Maxine's face on the front cover of the brochure, with its taut, perfectly made-up skin and long blonde hair pulled straight back in a severe ponytail. I kept trying to picture her and Mona as young 20-something Californians in New York. They looked a bit like yin and yang versions of each other. Both impeccably dressed and striking, but Mona was the more natural beauty. The thick shock of black hair she'd had when I was young had since morphed into a stunning shade of silver. Maxine, on the other hand, had a façade that looked like it came with a lot of work, her porcelain face and highlighted hair masking whatever was going on beneath. She also looked older than Mona, even though I knew they were the same age. Still, there she was on the cover of the program, standing on the terrace outside the room where she died holding a martini glass like the one found next to her on the bathtub. *What happened to you, Maxine?* I thought, as I put the brochure in my bag and headed out of the hotel, just as Maxine had done the day she disappeared.

CHAPTER EIGHT

As I started walking in the direction of Central Park, I took a closer look at the outside of the hotel, which stretched all the way to 5th Avenue. At the corner, I looked up to see if I could see the Penthouse Suite terrace that looked in that direction, but it was too high. I did note what appeared to be a security camera attached to one of the awnings on the second floor.

I then checked to see if there was an entrance on the 5th Avenue side of the building. It looked like there had been at one point. I found an ornate metal door embedded in the building's brick façade with an elegant plaque noting the entrance around the corner. There was no handle so I tried pushing the door, but it didn't budge—either sealed off or locked up tight from the inside. If my bearings were correct, it would have opened onto the hall on the side of the hotel near the elevators. Even if you somehow gained access from this side of the building, it's not like you could slip in without anyone seeing. I made a mental note to check with Leonora to see if there was a way to access the hotel from that side and also where the hotel might have other cameras hidden—that is, if anybody would let me near the footage from those cameras. (Unlikely!)

To the right of the hotel on 5th Avenue sat a very swank-looking building. Newer than The Françoise—maybe mid-20th century to the Françoise's early 20th century—and a lot taller. Like The Françoise, it had an awning, but the awning merely identified the address number. On a whim, I walked through the revolving door. Inside was a steel-gray foyer with an older man sitting on a tall chair behind a desk. Not dressed quite as fancy as Top Hat Renaldo, he still wore a navy-blue suit with little epaulets on the shoulder and a nametag that read "Bruno."

"May I help you?" the man asked. Not in the warmest tone, I have to say. Although I suppose it was to be expected. It wasn't a hotel so they weren't greeting guests.

"Maybe," I said with a smile that was not returned. I pulled out the conference guide and pointed to the picture of Maxine on it.

"Have you seen this woman recently?"

The man rolled his eyes. "As I told the last person who asked me that, no."

"Someone else came by?"

"A number of people, yes."

Chapter Eight

Huh, I thought. I didn't realize anyone had done any canvassing of the neighborhood, but I suppose Harriet could have sent some of the interns—sorry, ambassadors—in search of Maxine when she went AWOL.

"Okay," I said. "Thank you for your time." I started to turn toward the door, but then my curiosity got the best of me. "Is this an apartment building?" I asked.

"It's a co-op."

"Co-op," I said. "What's that mean? Like condos?"

Again, he rolled his eyes. He was going to get a serious eye strain if he kept that up. "Not condominiums. An individual owns a condo. A co-op is owned by the owners collectively with each unit worth a certain number of shares in the corporation that is the co-op."

He'd obviously said the words a lot before. And while they made sense individually, the concept seemed so alien to me that I wasn't quite sure what to make of it all. So, I just said, "Okay, thanks. Have a great day!"

"Yep" was all he said.

Back on 5th Avenue, I crossed over to Central Park. I was starting to run late so I took the first available path into the park. Roger was coming from his hotel on 8th Avenue in Midtown so we decided to meet at what appeared to be a halfway point. Looking at a map, I had found an entrance to the park on West 59th Street at 7th Avenue and decided that was as good a spot as any. As I walked in that direction, I felt a few butterflies in my stomach. I mean, I hadn't seen the guy in a couple of months, and our communication the past few days had been sketchy at best. Here I was in a city I didn't know talking to people I didn't know who said things like "co-op" and "bespoke." I hadn't gotten any sleep and was still dealing with the noise—have I mentioned the noise?—while also kind of reveling in the energy. Yeah, it was a lot.

I happily noted that I didn't have to walk all that far into the park to lose the street noise. *Kind of amazing how peaceful and bucolic the park is,* I thought as I meandered past a pond and went under a bridge on a circuitous route that led me to the southernmost edge of the park at 59th Street. The skyline on Central Park South was similar to that of the other sides, with one glaring exception—a few very narrow skyscrapers sticking up behind the beautiful older buildings. These weird towers rose at least a hundred stories and looked like they would topple over in a heavy wind. Coming from the land of earthquakes, it freaked me out just looking at them.

That freak-out feeling didn't last too long, as it was replaced by another when I looked down from the skyline and saw him: Roger. He was still pretty far in the distance, but that walk—kind of a tranquil amble—was unmistakable. Not sure if it was the balance developed from a lifetime of surfing or the swagger from his days based in Europe with the military police, but the man had a tendency to kind of float. He wasn't wearing the Hawaiian shirt that served as a uniform of sorts for Maui detectives. Instead, he had on a plain blue button-down shirt and suit jacket. I wondered who the Mona in his life was who curated an outfit that screamed "city detective." Maybe it was his

Chapter Eight

sister, the flight attendant who helped him out with the free flight benefits and made the cool leather-and-bone bracelets he wore—including the one he gave me. I felt my wrist to confirm it was still there. It had become a kind of talisman that grounded me in times of stress. And this was definitely one of those times.

When he got about 100 yards away, I could see a look of recognition—and a nod and a smile—when he saw me. As he got closer, the butterflies in my belly increased along with the spinning thoughts in my brain. I mean, again, we'd had a wonderful time together a couple months ago in Los Angeles, but now we were both out of our comfort zones: strange place, strange circumstances... although, to be fair, we first met under strange circumstances (dead body). Maybe that was our thing...

Like I said, spinning brain.

We were also very much out in public, although I had noticed even in my short time in the city that New Yorkers had a distinct tendency to conduct much of their private lives in public without any self-consciousness. When Roger was about 20 yards away, on the other side of a small path, I pondered what the greeting should be—hug? kiss? shake of the hand?

I then saw Roger start to obliviously cross the road in front of a woman running behind a very sleek-looking stroller with two dogs loping beside her. Behind her was a man race walking a half dozen dogs, followed by someone on a bike and a pedicab filled with tourists.

"Watch out!" I yelled, dashing in front of the stroller and knocking Roger back onto a grassy knoll.

"What the...?" he started to say.

"Hey, dude, I just saved your life," I said, laughing and pointing to the fast-moving pack. "If there is one thing I have learned, it's that New York ladies with strollers and dogs do not stop."

"Samantha Powers," Roger said, grinning and shaking his head as he sat up, "you never fail to amaze me."

We sat on the grass, smiling at each other for a moment. "So... How the hell are you?" he finally said.

"Aside from finding a dead body in the bathtub at a luxury hotel? Not bad," I said, looking around. "I actually kind of like this city."

Roger shrugged and grimaced.

"You don't?" I asked.

"I don't know. Let's face it, it's about as far as you can get from Hawaii in every possible way. I mean, the noise alone..." I laughed that he had noticed it too. "Add to that the fact I've been trapped for two days in a hotel conference center with hundreds of other cops and forensics scientists—not to mention my boss."

"The Maui chief of police?"

"Yes, Chief Akiona." He nervously looked at the time on his phone. "The truth is I haven't seen the city. To me, it's just been meeting rooms and cop talk."

"Yikes."

"Yikes, indeed," Roger said, sounding a lot more like someone who might say yikes than Mona did. He pointed to the grass and trees that surrounded us. "You know, I think this is the first time I've even seen the color green since I've been here."

"It's nice, right?"

✦ Chapter Eight ✦

Roger nodded. "Much needed." He took a long breath in. "Sorry if I've been a little short in my texts."

"No worries. I get it," I lied. But it was a benign sort of lie, don't you think?

"Thanks."

"How long of a break do you have?" I asked.

He looked at his phone again. "I have to be at a session on footprint analysis in two hours."

"About the same here, except for the part about the footprint analysis." Happily, that got a laugh. "I have to go and pick up my stuff at Tina's brownstone. Get this: I'm moving into The Françoise Hotel."

"Fancy."

"You betcha." I thought for a moment. "So… you up for a small New York adventure?"

"Maybe," Roger said. Then he looked at me, and as if realizing we hadn't had a proper greeting, took my face in his hands and pulled me in for a kiss.

"Hello, Sam," he whispered.

"Well, hello Kula," I said, using his Hawaiian name and taking his hand in mine. Suddenly, all was right with the world (except for the death of Maxine, of course). But first things first: "Have you tried the pizza here yet?"

I took Roger to my new favorite spot, Aldo's Pizza. Okay, so it was the only spot I knew. There, I introduced him to real New York pizza, which he agreed was pretty spectacular, and filled him in on everything that had happened since I arrived. From the disappearance and death of Maxine Martinique to the characters I'd met at Tina's (sue me, I may have omitted Hunky Hastings) to the crazy closet room I had been staying in to the super fancy Françoise Hotel with its own cast of characters. I then told him about my new assignment to write about the hotel and the city—and the things I overheard in Georg's office.

"Wow," Roger said, wiping the exquisite pizza juices off his face in a way that made me want to lick them off myself. (The city was obviously having an effect on my libido.) "You've seen a lot more of New York than I have."

"I get around," I said, shrugging and smiling. We tossed our paper plates in the trash, walked back to 5th Avenue, and headed downtown. He took my hand, which I loved, even if it now required us to synchronize our moves around the crowds of pedestrians.

"Fighting this," Roger said, motioning toward the hordes of people, "on a daily basis would drive me crazy."

"Don't get that on Maui, huh?"

"Maybe at one of the festivals in Kaanapali, but the throngs there are more benign."

"And you've got the ocean as an outlet."

"That we do." He smiled at me. "We've got to get you back there, you know."

"I would not be opposed to that at all," I said. We walked a little farther before I finally asked, "So, any thoughts on Maxine's death?"

Roger thought for a moment. "I'm going to be honest here, Sam. From everything you've told me, it sounds like an accidental drowning."

"But what about the vial—the keta-something I saw? No mention by the coroner."

Chapter Eight

"Could be ketamine. Some people like to spray or snort it."

"You've read up on it."

"It's become a popular party drug. We even had a session on it. The problem is it's used both legally and illegally. People take it to battle depression, usually intravenously and monitored in a therapist's office. Its dissociative effects also make it popular as a party drug, so people acquire it illegally. But even if that was the case, they don't usually prosecute that stuff—high-profile deaths like the actor Matthew Perry's aside. And it still wouldn't indicate foul play if that's what you are thinking."

"I don't know what I'm thinking," I said honestly. "I just keep coming back to the fact that the woman went AWOL and then somehow snuck back into the hotel without anyone knowing just to die in the bathtub."

"That is odd. I'll give you that. Maybe now that you are staying in the hotel, you can figure out how that happened."

By then, we had reached Rockefeller Center. We walked away from the throngs on 5th to take it all in.

"This isn't too bad, right? Kind of cool to see it in person, right?"

"I suppose," Roger admitted. "I mean, I did kind of like the TV show *30 Rock*."

"How about *Saturday Night Live* or *Elf*? They all happened right here," I said, laughing. "We're in the center of the universe, baby."

Roger gave a slight smile and squeezed my hand.

"I need to go this way," he said, pointing east. "Back to the hotel o' cops."

"And I need to go that way," I said, pointing west. "To the brownstone o' dancers."

"Yeah, I know."

"So... will we get to see each other again while you're here?" I asked.

"I'll try. It's hard, though," he said. "Especially with my boss..."

"The chief."

"The chief," he said, nodding. "Here with me."

"I get it. I do." I didn't really. *C'mon, man, slip out of your hotel at night! Be adventurous.* But I didn't say that. Maybe I should have.

"If I can, I will," he said. "I promise."

Roger gave my hand another squeeze and kissed me—right there in the middle of Rockefeller Center! Look at us with the NYC PDA!—before saying, "As long as you promise to be careful." He tipped his forehead to mine and looked deep into my eyes. "Okay?"

"Always," I said with a bit of a smile. Okay, I hadn't always been as careful as I should. But this was different. I was just going to do some asking around, and mostly for my story, right? I waved goodbye and started walking back to Tina's to pick up my bag and move over to The Françoise, where the Business of Luxury conference was about to begin.

CHAPTER NINE

With a bit more pep in my step, I made my way back to Tina's brownstone. It was a gorgeous spring day, and I enjoyed the walk, discovering tons of shops and restaurants, and hello, have you ever seen the inside of Grand Central Terminal? Amazing! Around every corner, there was a new discovery to be had. I felt a buzz and a life force I hadn't felt in a long time. I was also starting to understand why the locals got upset at us clueless tourists. Did you know that some of them just obliviously stop right in the middle of where you're walking? Come on, people, keep it moving!

As I reached Tina's brownstone, I saw Hastings walking out of a wrought-iron gate located below the steps. Ah, so this was the basement apartment Tina had mentioned. I'd noticed other basement units on my walks, some bearing signs for businesses like hair salons or dog grooming or daycare. Made me wonder just what they looked like.

"Hi, Hastings," I called.

"Oh, hey Sam, how's it going?" Hastings asked with that cute, cute smile of his.

"It's going well," I said. "I'm actually coming to pick up my things and move over to The Françoise Hotel."

"Oooh, fancy," he said.

"The fanciest. Totally my style," I said with a wave at my totally not fancy outfit. I added a curtsy like the one he and Tina liked to pull out. "Is this your place?"

"It is indeed." He gave a wave at the gate and added a little curtsy as well. Flirting, right? Was he (were we?) flirting? There was a pause, and then he picked up on the fact I was dying of curiosity. "Did you want to check it out?"

"Do you mind? All these spaces you New Yorkers have tucked here and there kind of fascinate me."

"Not sure how fascinating it is," Hastings said. "But come on. Happy to show you."

We walked down the stairs, through the gate, and then down a few more stairs. There, past the front door, I saw a large living area with exposed brick walls and a floor that appeared to be concrete decorated with throw rugs and a hodgepodge of furniture to create an all-in-one living/dining area with a kitchenette against the wall. A hall in the back held a few doorways.

"Nice digs," I said.

"Thank you. As you may have guessed, much of this furniture came from shows that Aunt Tina danced in or choreographed. When the shows ran a long time,

Chapter Nine

they'd have to replace some of the sets. Tina offered to take the furniture to help fill the brownstone." He pointed to an ornate couch that appeared to have been recently recovered. "The King and I." To a mid-century modern dining room table. "Bye, Bye Birdie." And a hat rack. "Chicago."

"Cool," I said.

"Very. I never got to see Aunt Tina dance on Broadway—she'd retired and started the studio by the time I was born—but it's fun to have these souvenirs."

I turned to the wall facing the street and noticed the only windows were at the very top. I saw a wide variety of shoes walking by outside. Plus, of course, stroller wheels with dogs following along.

"Must be a trip watching the city walk by every day," I said.

"I guess it is," he said, as we heard some tap tap tapping going on above us. He smiled. "That would be the 4 p.m. dance class letting out."

"Never a dull moment, eh?"

"Not here, although luckily my bedroom in the back is quiet, and it opens up to a small patio garden."

"I thought I saw some plants down there from my window in the kitchen room," I said. "Very cool. It's like you all have everything you need but in a very small space. In a way, it's not unlike our family home in Carmel, except that I'm above a garage instead of under a house."

"Probably less prone to flooding in serious rain storms," Hastings said, pointing to the doorway leading to the front stairs. "A problem when you're literally underground." Ah, the cement floor now made sense.

"That is true," I said. "But we currently have a pretty serious leak over the kitchen counter."

"Splash blocks help. I use them along the windows and the front door."

"I'll have to remember that."

"Here to help." Hastings smiled and looked at a clock on the wall above my head. "Hate to rush off, but I need to get to the theater."

"Oh, sorry to hold you up. Thank you for giving me the tour."

"Such that it is," Hastings said, closing the door behind us as we made our way back up to the sidewalk. "We're going to miss having you around, you know."

"I've only been here for two days."

"And it's been a very pleasurable two days."

Again with the flirting. Aren't I having the most amazing day for getting attention from cute men? I may have blushed. "Well, I'm still in the city and will be here until the end of the conference. I'm sure you will see me around here and there."

"I hope so." And with that he smiled, turned and walked down the street, giving a small hop as he did. Man, he was cute. Sorry, Roger, but he was, and I had to admit all the male attention added to the buzz I was getting from the city.

I didn't find anyone home on the main floor of the brownstone—not even another dance class in progress—so I packed up my bag, left a thank-you note for Tina on the breakfast nook in the kitchen, and started over to The Françoise. I decided to grab a cab. I was

★ Chapter Nine ★

lugging my suitcase and didn't want a repeat of the sweaty mess I was when I first got into town. I was, after all, checking into The Françoise. Not to mention, according to my phone, I had already walked more than five miles between my trek across Central Park and back down to Tina's. Plus, I got to wave down my first cab! How hip was that?

Before long, I was dropped off at the front door of The Françoise. When I entered the lobby, it was still bustling with people checking in at the front desk and with the ambassadors at the Business of Luxury table. I nodded at Top Hat Renaldo as he helped someone with their bags. He looked at me and pointed at my bag to ask if I needed help. I shook my head no, and he offered a tip of his cap in return. Saucy. I then walked down the hall and over to the elevator, where I found Leonora waiting at "my" elevator.

"Good afternoon, Leonora."

"Good afternoon, Ms. Powers," she said.

"Please, Sam."

"Good afternoon, Sam. I heard you were joining us. Welcome."

"Thank you."

Before I got into the elevator, I looked down the hall and saw the door I'd spotted on 5th Avenue. It looked sealed up even from here.

"Hey, what's the deal with that door?" I asked, pointing to the end of the hall.

Leonora looked. "The 5th Avenue door?"

"Yeah, I saw it earlier today and was wondering about it. Was it ever an entrance?"

"It was. Before the renovations. The new ownership decided they preferred everyone enter via the 63rd Street entrance so they sealed it up."

"It doesn't open at all?"

"No."

"How long have you worked here, Leonora?"

"Thirty-five years."

"Wow. That's impressive."

"They treat us very well. We've had very little turnover."

"Does the new ownership change anything?"

Leonora offered an enigmatic smile and a non-answer: "We've always been a family here."

Discretion still your middle name, eh? I decided to switch tactics. "So, is the 63rd Street entrance the only entrance?"

"Except for the service entrance, of course."

"Where is that entrance? I've only seen the main entrance and that sealed door on 5th Avenue."

"It's pretty well hidden," Leonora said with a smile. "There's a small service alley halfway between 5th and Madison. A door there leads into the operations department and then down into the basement level. Makes it easier to get deliveries in and out of the kitchen."

"That's the same level as the show office?"

"Yes. Our locker room and commissary are also on that level but kept separate from the meeting rooms down there."

Interesting. "Thanks."

"Happy to help in any way I can," Leonora said with a brighter smile. They were so helpful, these

Chapter Nine

Françoise employees—as long as the questions weren't too probing. All that darn discretion.

With that, we had reached the 7th floor. As I exited the elevator, I looked up and saw a security camera, but before I could ask about it, a bell indicated that someone had summoned the elevator. I thanked Leonora and headed down the hall to my room. When I passed Mona's door, I pondered knocking. At some point, I wanted to get her alone so she could give me the answers to all the questions I had but decided it could wait. I mean, I wasn't sure where she was and even if she was in her room; maybe she needed some space. I continued on down to my room, which was— as Candace had indicated—right next door. I used the key card she'd handed me, got the green light and click that meant it was open, and went inside.

The room was... how do I say this? Amazing. Even though it was a standard room with a king bed, it certainly lived up to its Royal King moniker, and offered at least three times the space as the closet-sized room I had at Tina's. I could even swing my arms and not touch walls. I reveled in the expansiveness while also noting the locked door on my right that adjoined Mona's suite. I then saw the little panel in the wall next to the front door where you could push "do not disturb," remembering that it was lit when we had entered Maxine's room. Hmmm. I pushed the red dot. Curious if it looked the same, I reopened the front door and peeked into the hall side of the wall. Yep, lit up just like Maxine's. Hmmm. Who could have done that, if it wasn't her? Or, if it was her, why didn't anybody see her entering the hotel?

These questions could all wait while I continued my spin around the room and through the very spacious bathroom before returning. Not unlike the dancers I saw in Tina's studio, I did a pirouette before falling onto the bed, which was huge—at least three times the one I'd been sleeping on and covered in the softest duvet I'd ever felt. This lap of luxury, as it were, felt good.

CHAPTER TEN

I enjoyed the comfort of my bed for maybe ten minutes before I heard a knock at the door that adjoined Mona's suite.

"Sam," I heard Mona say in a muffled voice from the other side, "I thought I heard your door. Are you there?"

"I'm here," I called as I walked over. I unlocked the deadbolt and then turned the knob to open the door. Mona stood on the other side of her door, which had a similar configuration. "Hello, neighbor."

Mona laughed, and then looked at my outfit. It was the same one I'd put on to start the day, which was beginning to look a little rumpled after all my walks through the city. Before I could say anything, she said, "Come in. It's time to get you dressed for the opening reception."

"But I brought…" I started to say, pointing to my suitcase. Mona threw me a look. "Of course, if you have something else in mind…" I continued.

I followed Mona into the living area of her suite, where I found a bustle of activity. Harriet was sitting in the middle of the room having her hair and makeup done by a tall man with spiky purple hair that matched his purple-patterned coat. Nearby, another Mona-sized (a.k.a. tall, lean) woman with gorgeous ebony-colored skin, black hair slicked back into a severe bun, and a long silver scarf sorted through a rack of clothes, looking back at Harriet occasionally while she did. Between the similarities in height and impeccable fashion sense, they seemed to represent Mona in her native habitat, with me the small, poorly dressed interloper who happened upon them.

"She's next," Mona said to the woman, pointing to me. "Sam, this is Nadine. Nadine, Sam."

"Nice to meet you," I said, to which Nadine gave the briefest of eyebrow lift nods.

"Nadine was one of the stylists I worked with at *Vogue*," Mona said. "We pulled her in to help Harriet become fabulous before she makes her speech at the event tonight."

"I don't want to make a speech," Harriet whined.

"Without Maxine, I'm afraid you are now the face and voice of the conference, my dear."

"I don't want to be the face and voice of the conference," Harriet whined but somewhat quieter. She looked at me and whispered, "I'm much happier in the background."

"I hear you," I said.

Chapter Ten

"Luckily, we found everything we need from the suppliers exhibiting at the conference—hair products, makeup, clothing," Mona said, touching some of the dresses. "This is a lovely line."

"It's Richonda's," Nadine said. "One of the lines Chartreuse is representing here."

"She's outdone herself," Mona said. "Where'd she source the fabrics? These patterns are divine."

"A small textile shop started by a French couple in Hoboken of all places."

While they continued speaking in *Vogue*-talk, I turned to Harriet.

"How are you doing?"

Harriet sighed. "As well as can be expected, I suppose," she said.

"Is there anything I can help you with?"

"You're so sweet. No, I think we have everything under control. Dmitri is down overseeing the room setups with the ambassadors. And Mona's been a godsend, of course—as always."

As always? What the heck did that mean? Everybody I had met (with the exception of Hastings) had such a long history, it was like they spoke in code. The two of us watched Mona still chatting away with Nadine about the clothes on the rack, and I realized there was so much I did not know about her.

"Have you known Mona a long time?" I asked.

Harriet nodded. "I met Mona and Maxine around the same time. When I first came to the city from upstate, I was a receptionist at BBDO."

"BBDO?"

"Big Madison Avenue advertising agency."

"Ah." I nodded.

"I worked in the TV production department but wasn't given much to do beyond answering the phone and taking messages. I wanted something more interesting but wasn't sure what. Then I met Maxine. She was an account exec making the move to public relations. When she started her own firm, she asked if I wanted to join her. I immediately said, 'yes.'"

Harriet offered a rueful smile. "It wasn't always smooth, and I had to deal with a lot. A lot," she said, looking me in the eye for emphasis. "But it was always exciting. For a nobody like me from the Hudson Valley with a husband deployed overseas, it was exciting. I felt kind of honored she'd picked me, you know? Even better, through her I met Tina, and Mona and Victor and Winston and Scarlet and… Well, you know. They all became my family." Another rueful smile. Then she brightened. "The best thing about Maxine is that she had no desire to micromanage. She left me alone to run the company and spent her time finding the newest, latest thing." Harriet had tears in her eyes. "I mean, Maxine had her moments—recently more often…" Another sigh. "Still hard for me to believe she's gone."

I felt for her while also wanting to follow up with oh-so-many questions but was interrupted by Mona saying, "Now, this one is perfect for Sam…"

"This what?" I asked, looking over to see Mona holding up a slinky black print dress that was definitely not my style. "Yeah, I don't think so," I said.

"Oh yes, Sam," Mona said. "Time to show off that cute little figure of yours."

★ Chapter Ten ★

"I thought you said the reception was business casual. I brought a skirt."

"A skirt that's great for California but not New York."

Nadine gave my outfit a once-over. "You Californians do love your cotton, don't you?"

Uh, well, yeah. Why wouldn't we?

"Just for tonight. For me," Mona said, holding out the silk dress.

I looked at Mona. What I wouldn't do for this woman. "Fine," I said, holding my arms out like a scarecrow. "Do what you will."

An hour later, I headed down the hall in my clingier-than-I-would-have-liked dress and a pair of heels over Carmel's legal limit, with my hair blown out and face made up in a way that was most definitely not, well, me. When I got to the elevator, it was not Leonora waiting for me but an older balding man wearing thick black glasses.

"Hello, Ms. Powers," he said, offering a small bow. Again, just so, so formal, these Françoise folks.

"Hello, uh, Otto," I said, reading the nametag on his uniform, which was somewhat similar to Leonora's white shirt and vest but with an added black suit jacket similar to the one the concierges wore. "We haven't met before, have we?"

"No, we have not. I am the swing shift operator."

"And yet you know my name."

"You came out of 736. I know who is staying in 736."

It really did not seem possible to sneak anything by these employees at The Françoise. "Well, it's nice to meet you then," I said.

"Likewise. Are you heading down to the reception?"

"I am."

"Ms. Reynolds went down about 15 minutes ago," he said. Great, Mona was probably already wondering why I was late, but I had to take a few selfies in the mirror, right? Lizzy and Uncle Henry would get a kick out of me in this getup. I was still deciding if I should send one to Roger.

As we headed down, I decided to see if I could glean any information. "So, have you been working this same shift the past week?"

"At times."

"I don't suppose you saw Maxine Martinique go into her room in the penthouse."

Otto offered a perfunctory smile. "We do not speak of other guests at The Françoise, Ms. Powers."

"Yes, I've heard. Discretion is your middle name and all. But even friends of guests? Friends of guests who, you know, died?"

Otto gave me another smile, but it was a closed-lip smile that said nothing, as did he until we reached the lobby. He pulled back the gates.

"Enjoy your evening, Ms. Powers."

"Thank you, Otto," I said, immediately giving him the nickname Officious Otto.

Man, these hotel people were hard to crack. I get that it was their *thing,* but come on. As I stepped out of the elevator, I could already hear the buzz of voices coming from the lobby. I found the conference

Chapter Ten

check-in table with the oh-so-young Business of Luxury ambassadors.

"Hey there, how's it going?" I asked. In return, I got the weirdest stares.

"I'm sorry. Do we know you?" one of them asked in, I have to say, the snottiest tone possible.

"Sam. Samantha Powers. Harriet and Mona's friend. I met you all yesterday down in the show office."

"Yeah, I don't think so," another said, in the second snottiest tone possible.

Do I really look so different, or are they just assholes?

"Okay, whatever," I said. *Hey, you want snark, I can give you snark.* "I'm guessing I should have a name badge? Harriet said she left one for me."

One of them looked through the badges left on the table. "Oh, yeah, here it is."

"Thank you, oh so much," I said in a way I hoped was dripping with disdain while also rolling my eyes. Business of Luxury, my ass.

I draped the dark blue lanyard over my neck, noting that it had been emblazoned with the New York City Tourism logo, and headed toward the ballroom. As I entered, I was surprised to find Tina, Winston, Scarlet, and Victor standing next to Mona in a corner, surveying the crowd now mingling amid the tabletop displays I had watched being set up earlier that day.

"My, my, don't we dress up well?" Scarlet said as I walked over to them.

"Stunning," Winston said. I may have blushed.

"Oh, you beautiful girl," Tina said, pulling me into a hug.

"Mona did this to me," I said, pointing to her looking smug as hell, in addition to being quite the fashion plate herself. I took everyone in, all dressed in what I guessed was their version of "cocktail" attire: Tina in a flowing and very shimmering dress, Scarlet and Vincent in his-and-hers suits (they weren't matching, but they weren't not matching if that makes sense), and Winston wearing a sassy cravat.

"You all dress up nice yourselves. I didn't realize you would be here."

"We're always here," Scarlet said with a sigh.

"How many conferences is it now?" Winston asked.

"I don't want to count."

"Oh, come on, it's not like it's a trial to be wined and dined at The Françoise," Tina said.

"How is it going?" I asked.

"Things seem to be proceeding as well as can be expected," Mona said as a server came by with a tray of sparkling-pink-liquid-filled champagne glasses. "Drink?"

"I'd love one," I said. "Thank you." I nodded to the server and took a swig of the bubbly. "Yum."

"Moët," said Winston, nodding as if that meant anything to me.

"Has to be Veuve," Victor corrected him.

"Oh, please, you snobs," Scarlet said. "It's a winery from a new appellation Maxine found just outside the Champagne region in France. They make a sparkling rosé from a blend of grenache and pinot grapes. Their distributor is a vendor." She nodded to a table filled with wine bottles across the way. "We got it at cost."

"Of course," Mona said as the others nodded.

Chapter Ten

Whatever the hell it was, I will say it was *delish*. Before I knew it, another server came by with a tray containing small bites of something in large white serving spoons.

"The ahi tartare is to die for," Winston said, nodding at the tray. He then noticed everyone's astonished faces. "What?"

"She's been dead for less than 48 hours," Scarlet said.

"We all deal with tragedy in our own way," Winston said, leaning down to me. "Mine's with humor."

"Mine, too," I whispered back. "Gets me in trouble."

Winston nodded toward Scarlet. "Me, too," he whispered. Then said, more loudly, "Try one, Sam. They're delicious."

I took one of the spoons and slurped down the concoction. It was quite tasty, if perhaps not "to die for," given the circumstances. As I placed the spoon back on the tray (as everyone indicated I should), I took a closer look around the room. It was bustling, with people eating, drinking, and chatting, both in the middle of the room and at the 20-or-so tabletop exhibits lining the walls. I saw my new friend Nikki, with Bespoke Travel Adventures, who waved when she caught my eye.

"I see you met Nikki," Mona said, suddenly by my side.

"I did, earlier today when they were setting up."

"She's a good person for you to know. Her company offers wonderful luxury-market trips that we should be covering in the magazine."

"They are top-notch," Victor said, one of the few times I'd heard the man speak. "We took their trip along the Camino de Santiago."

"You walked the Camino?" Mona asked.

"Oh, no, we visited the five-star paradors in towns along the Camino," Scarlet said.

"We're not animals, Mona," Victor said.

"No, we are not," Scarlet said, and the two of them shared a toast and a grin.

"I'll make sure to talk to her more in the next few days," I said, laughing and taking another sip of the elixir that was the sparkling rosé (whatever the hell the label).

"Oh, look, Harriet's about to give the opening remarks," Scarlet said.

I turned to see Harriet walking onto the stage wearing a vibrant blue dress, her hair pulled up in a glittery barrette and face made up in a way that enhanced her features. Wow. Talk about a transformation. She could teach Clark Kent a thing or two, except that, similar to Superman's change in appearance, the transformation was less about a change in her looks than attitude—from obsequious to confident.

Harriet took the mic from Dmitri, tapped it a few times, and said, "Hello all!" After a minute or two, the crowd quieted down and turned to look at her. Dmitri stepped to the side as Harriet moved to the center of the stage.

"Welcome to the Business of Luxury," Harriet said with a big smile that lit up her face. She patted her heart. "I am so happy to see all of you gathered here, especially after such a heartbreaking few days." She

Chapter Ten

looked down and took a deep breath in what became a moment of silence for Maxine. To the assembled crowd's credit, so did they.

When she had their rapt attention, Harriet looked back up and continued: "I'd like to think that Maxine is looking down on us and smiling at the wonderful community we've created." Harriet raised her champagne glass. "And so, as we toast Maxine, I will begin as she always did by saying, 'Here's to the Business of Luxury.'" Harriet took a sip, as did everyone else.

I looked over at Mona, Tina, Winston, Victor, and Scarlet, and then back to the stage, where I noticed Georg and a woman I didn't recognize now standing near Dmitri. The woman, who grasped Georg's arm in a very proprietary way, was dripping in gold and diamonds. While she looked to be about Mona's age, she had the super taut skin and puffy lips of someone who spent a lot of time with an aesthetician (or, let's be honest, plastic surgeon). Even more than I'd noticed with Maxine's picture on the cover of the conference program, Mona's natural beauty outshone hers in every way, if you asked me. Not that anyone was asking me.

"I would like to thank all our wonderful hosts..." Harriet continued, gesturing toward Georg and Desiree, "...and our speakers, and of course, our sponsors..." At this point, Harriet named off a ridiculously long list of sponsors. "...for continuing to support us during this trying time."

Harriet again briefly bowed her head before continuing with a confident smile. I have to say, she was expertly working this crowd. "We have a great lineup of programming scheduled for the next two days: education sessions, field trips to some of New York's most iconic sites, and of course, the scheduled meetings with our wonderful vendors. In a half hour, we will be offering anyone who's interested a tour of the hotel. As I'm sure you've already noticed, the renovations made following the acquisition by Hotels du Jour are quite simply stunning." She again motioned toward Georg and Desiree. Each gave a nod and wave.

"This is your chance to see them up close," Harriet continued. "You can meet The Françoise's Candace Berkley at their tabletop near the entrance." Harriet pointed to Candace in the back, who gave a big happy wave quite unlike the more royal-type wave of Georg and Desiree. "Until then, I'll let you all get back to it. But again, I would like to extend my deepest appreciation for your support and your love of this conference that has meant so much to me and to Maxine, may she rest in peace."

Harriet put her hand back over her heart as everyone applauded. Harriet wore a big smile on her face, and as they say in New York, a star was born.

CHAPTER ELEVEN

The next morning when I heard the alarm on my phone go off, I woke up groggily and took a look around. The good news was that instead of sleeping curled up against a wall with a sweater wrapped around my head to keep the morning light and sounds of the city at bay, I was ensconced in a king-sized bed under a sumptuous duvet in a room with black-out curtains and what I'm guessing was double-paned glass as it was absolutely silent. Amazing. In a perfect world, I would have spent a good few hours lounging in this lap of luxury. Unfortunately, I had to make it downstairs by 9 a.m. to see Mona speak on her panel. That wouldn't have been so bad had I made it back to my room at a reasonable hour. I had not.

Still on California time, I got a second wind after the hotel tour, which mostly just covered the places Mona and I had visited the day before. The one place

I hadn't seen was the rooftop bar, which we reached using the designated elevator in the lobby lounge. I found Officious Otto now serving as a bouncer of sorts just outside. I gave him a nod, which he returned as the group Candace was leading trooped into the elevator.

When we reached the top, the elevator opened onto a small hallway that led out to a large terrace surrounded by big brick archways. The view of the city through the open-air archways was spectacular, although the wind at that height added a chill to the air. A bar had been added to one side of the terrace, with couches and high-top tables sprinkled about.

"Like many other hotels in the city, we realized this terrace would be perfect for a rooftop bar," said Candace. "It was part of the penthouse apartment the original owner built in the early 1900s. His descendants kept this floor as their private space until they sold the building to Hotels du Jour."

Candace pointed to the hall where the elevator dropped us off. "That hall used to lead into the living quarters, but it has been sealed off."

I looked over at the edge of the building, where there was a tall black gate. If I wasn't mistaken, that was the same gate I'd seen on the small patio outside the master bedroom—sorry, primary bedroom—where Maxine had died. As if reading my mind (or just following my gaze), Candace continued.

"We also locked the gate that adjoins the Penthouse Suite, which as you all know, is where we had planned to offer conference hospitality …"

Not possible when it's covered in police tape, I thought.

Chapter Eleven

"...luckily, the weather for the next two days looks good, so we will be setting everything up out here since this bar doesn't open until 5 p.m. anyway."

As the attendees made happy murmuring noises, I looked around at the regular bar crowd cheerfully mingling away. They mostly looked to be young professional types. Just the types I might be hanging out with myself if I lived in the city, I realized, wondering what my life would look like if that were the case.

I followed the group back to the elevator, where Candace nodded to another hotel employee who then pushed the button for us. They sure took their elevator security seriously at The Françoise.

Back down in the lounge, the attendees began to disperse.

"Thanks for the tour," I said to Candace.

"Of course," she said. "If there's anything else you want to see, just let me know. These old hotels have a lot of nooks and crannies."

"I'm starting to see that," I said, laughing as we exited the elevator and saw Nikki sitting on one of the couches in the lounge.

"Hey there, you two," Nikki said, waving. "Want to join me for a drink? Patty and Leopold from Furry Companion Bijouterie—or whatever they're calling their bougie doggie jewelry company—have those two seats, but there's plenty of room here."

Candace and I looked at each other and both said, "Sure!" I mean, I had the slinky dress on. I should get some mileage out of it, right?

"Feel free to order whatever you want at the bar and tell Julio to put it on my account," Candace said.

"Are you sure?" I asked.

"Absolutely," she said, taking a seat next to Nikki. "It's business! If you could tell him I'd love my usual, that would be great."

"Happy to."

I walked up to the bar, thinking that what I needed to complete my image as the quintessential New Yorker was a martini. Of course, when I got there, I realized I had no idea how to order one. I didn't think one just said, "Martini." There are specific ways—more than "shaken, not stirred"—right? Based on how the crowd at Tina's discussed Maxine's exact way of ordering them, I had no idea how to do that. I decided it didn't hurt just to admit it.

"Hello, Ms. Powers," the hip-looking young man behind the bar said. Before I could ask how he knew my name (and becoming a bit paranoid that the workers at The Françoise seemed to know my every move), I realized I still had my nametag on a lanyard around my neck.

"And hello to you, Julio," I said, noting his nametag along with his huge smile, curly brown hair, and series of diamond studs on both his ear lobes.

"What's your pleasure?"

"Well, Candace said to tell you she would like her usual," I said, pointing to her on the couch. Hipster Julio looked in her direction and she waved. He nodded.

"Got it."

"If you don't mind my asking, what is her usual?" I asked.

Chapter Eleven

"Miss Candace is partial to a rye Manhattan straight up with three dashes of bitters," he said.

I'm not sure I knew what any of those words meant.

"And how about you? What can I get you?" he asked, starting to make her drink by picking and choosing from among the incredible array of barware, bottles, and garnishes surrounding him.

I decided to come clean. "Well, I'm thinking I might like a martini," I started, "but I'm going to be honest and say I have no idea how I'd like it made."

"Would you like me to make you the Françoise's signature version?"

"Perfect," I said. "What is that? Just so I know."

"We use our house vodka, which is Laporte, with a whiff of dry vermouth, orange bitters, and a lemon twist."

"Okay, hit me," I said. And then figured why not prod a bit. "I heard that Maxine Martinique had a very specific martini."

He raised his eyebrows. "She did indeed."

"Do you really remember everyone's drink?"

"I try, especially with our regular guests. Maxine was here often enough during the planning of the conference that I got to know her specifications."

"And they were?"

"Dry, dirty Bonheur vodka martini up with exactly three olives."

"What's Bonheur?"

Julio held up a striking emerald green bottle with a silver label that read, "Bonheur."

"And dry means?"

"Dash of dry vermouth."

"How does that differ from the Françoise version?"

"We use a whiff of vermouth."

"Is a whiff drier than dry?" I asked, truly confused.

"Just a whiff drier, yes," he said with a smile as he handed me my drink.

I took a sip. It was fine, I suppose, if a little industrial to my tastes, which tended toward Monterey County wines or the bubbly we had earlier. I took my drink and Candace's and joined what had become a dozen or so people sitting on the couches in the corner. Many of them seemed to be on the same conference circuit or had mutual acquaintances and were chatting away like old friends. I sat in the space Candace and Nikki had saved between them.

"Welcome," Nikki said, toasting her drink.

I clinked my glass against hers and Candace's before saying, "Thank you again for the tour, but I'm still hoping at some point for something more extensive."

"You want to know all our little secrets, don't you?" she asked, laughing and taking a big sip of her drink. Hell, she chugged the thing.

"I guess I just want to get to know more about what makes The Françoise special," I said, smiling as I took a sip of my martini. Still industrial, but I managed to choke the sip down and felt the warmth slide down my insides. "You know, like I did with the Mokihana Resort in Maui." I hoped mentioning the article she told me she liked might get her to open up.

"Well," Candace said, sounding a little tipsier. "I'm not sure if you heard, but discretion…"

Chapter Eleven

"...is our middle name," I helped her finish, as did Nikki.

Candace and Nikki both giggled and said, "Shhh" at the same time. Yep, they were both getting tipsy.

"Is that how it is at all the hotels where you've worked?" I continued, hoping to get something out of either of them, especially in their inebriated state.

"Yes and no," Candace said.

"Hotels kind of run the gamut," Nikki said, "but in general, the more expensive or exclusive, the more discreet."

"Definitely," Candace said. "Not sure if you know this, Sam, but one of the reasons hotels don't call to let you know you left something behind is that our guests aren't always where they're supposed to be."

I thought about it for a moment. "Oh, so like someone leaves a message saying, 'Mr. Smith, you left your watch behind,' and Mrs. Smith didn't know he was there."

"Exactly," Nikki said.

"Discretion is our middle name," Candace said, laughing again. "Be it the royal who likes to bring hookers into his room or the celebrity who likes to defecate in the shower."

"Ewwww!" Nikki said. "That one I hadn't heard."

"That was a few hotels ago. And, yes, eww. If I have learned one thing in this industry, it's that guests can be assholes."

"Now, now, discretion is your middle name," piped up Nikki.

Candace started giggling again. "And it's what they pay us the big bucks for, right?"

"Still, yuck," I said. I mean, really, yuck, right? But I realized I had a bit of an opening. "Anything like this happened before?"

"This?"

"You know, Maxine, dead bodies."

"Dead bodies galore. A few heart attacks with hookers. Or in a bathtub like Maxine, although hers was unexpected."

"In what way?"

"I don't know. I mean, Maxine was eccentric, and yeah, she liked her vodka, but I never thought this would happen."

Candace got a sad look on her face. I didn't want her to close up, so I decided to prod just a little more. "Someone told me she'd gotten into ketamine."

"Oh god, who hasn't?" Nikki said, laughing again and lightening the mood.

"You knew Maxine did ketamine?"

"Everybody knew," said Candace. "She'd even been referring people to her doctor. Besides, it's probably safer than the vodka."

Unless you're doing it outside the doctor's office, which the vial next to the tub would indicate, I thought. Or maybe Roger was right, and it wasn't the smoking gun I thought it was. I decided to try a different tack.

"How often does Georg come into town?"

Candace rolled her eyes.

"Not a fan?"

She shrugged. "He's fine. I shouldn't say anything since he's the one who hired me."

"He hired you? It seems like most of the staff have been here forever."

Chapter Eleven

"That's true. They have. Hotels du Jour brought on a new executive team, but the rest came with the place, as they say—and they're great, I have to say. So great."

"And Georg?"

Candace again shrugged. "He's not here that often. He came in a few times to check on the progress of the renovations, but this is the first we've seen him since we reopened."

"I heard he's been gunning for the CEO job at Hotels du Jour," Nikki said.

"Where'd you hear that?" Candace snapped.

"I get around, Candace." Nikki smiled and took a sip from her drink.

"Oh, yeah, duh," Candace said, relaxing a bit. "Yes, that is the word on the street or around the hotel anyway. Georg has been married to Desiree forever, but from what I heard, she keeps him on a short leash and has been dangling the CEO gig ever since they met. Instead, the company has been sending him all over Europe to fix up troubled properties and acquire new ones. The last I heard from my general manager, who worked with Georg in Madrid, is that Desiree said he'd get the position if he could land The Françoise to help them expand the company's brand into the U.S. Now that he has and the renovation is a success, he's just waiting for the word."

"Is your general manager here this week?"

"No, Georg sent him to the corporate HQ in Paris for additional training. The truth is, I don't think he wanted another alpha dog on site."

"Is that his office Georg is using?"

"Yep." Candace leaned in. "Word has it that was Reginald Wentworth's original office."

"Oh really?" Nikki said, suddenly interested.

"Who's Reginald Wentworth?" I asked.

"The original owner. The guy who built the hotel back in the 1920s and lived in the penthouse apartment," Nikki said, and I realized I had seen his portrait in the lobby. "I recently read a book set in New York in the early 20th century where he was mentioned. He was known for running a secret drinking and gambling parlor at the height of Prohibition."

"Sounds like the first owner of the Lake Tahoe Lodge, which I recently wrote about for the magazine," I said, attempting to deflect any suspicion to my probing. "That's why I would love to learn more... you know, for my story."

"We'll see what we can do," Candace said, although she didn't seem to want any more questions. "I'm sure we have some literature around with more history of the hotel."

That was a stock answer if I ever heard one. *Back to "discretion is our middle name."*

Salacious stories and evasive answers aside, I have to say it was really great, this living the life of a New Yorker. I felt more energized than I had in a long time. Was it just four days earlier that I was feeling sorry for myself in Carmel? I was also starting to understand the whole "city that never sleeps" thing as I was decidedly not getting enough of the stuff (sleep, in case that wasn't clear). But who minded when there was so much fun to be had?

Chapter Eleven

As I lay in my bed continuing to mull the events of the night, I realized I may have even tipsy-texted Roger when I got back to my room at 1 a.m. and told him not to be such a stick-in-the-mud and come over and have his way with me. That thought bolted me out of bed. Oh, I hoped that hadn't really happened. I checked my phone. Thank god, I had written the text but not pushed "send" and could delete it as if it never happened. Whew. I guess. *Should I have sent it? Am I being too cautious with him? Is Lizzy right? Is he looking for more from me as much as I am from him?*

I lay back down in the bed and pondered just how long I could wait to get up before I would be late to Mona's session and where I'd packed my ibuprofen. I also came back to the reason I was there in the first place: Maxine. What happened to Maxine? Even with all the new information I'd gleaned, I still had no idea where she'd disappeared to and how she was able to sneak into the hotel only to die in the bathroom. I mean, yes, from what everyone had said, she could have gone to whoever her ketamine source was to get a boost, come back late at night through a secret entrance, added a vodka martini (or a bottle's worth), and slipped into oblivion. But she couldn't have done it all alone or unseen, so who might have helped her? For that, I either needed to talk a cop into getting a warrant to look at the security tapes (unlikely since they didn't seem to think a crime had been committed) or talk one of the hotel staff into confiding in me (also unlikely with their "discretion is our middle name" doctrine).

I also kept coming back to what the deal was between Mona and Georg. Or Georg and Maxine. Or Mona and Maxine. I wasn't sure why it mattered, except that between the vibes from the Tina gang and Georg's comment that some sort of secret had died with Maxine, I felt like I needed some answers. Mona had been evasive with me more than once since I'd been in New York—something she had never done before (that I knew of)—and I needed to find out why. Unfortunately, with the conference in full swing, getting Mona alone to ask would be a challenge.

CHAPTER TWELVE

I knew enough not to try to talk to Mona before her appearance on the panel but made sure I was in the Barrymore Room by 9 a.m. (sharp!). I grabbed a cup of coffee from the buffet in the back of the room and stood off to the side as Harriet took the stage, which was set with four chairs. I then noticed Spreadsheet Scarlet a few feet away to my right, scrolling through messages on her phone. I took a couple of steps in her direction.

"Good morning, Scarlet," I said quietly as people continued taking their seats.

Scarlet looked up at me through yet another pair of expensive-looking eyeglasses that matched her suit perfectly. "Oh, hello, Samantha."

"I'm surprised to see you here again."

"Just protecting my investment."

"Investment?"

Before I could probe further, Harriet began welcoming the crowd. I happily noticed it was a decent one, especially considering the number of people at the after-party in the lounge the night before. Harriet went over the day's schedule. Two education panels in the morning would be followed by a buffet lunch and personal appointments in the Gold Room. In the afternoon, an optional city tour set up by the tourism bureau would culminate with a reception and artist talk at Victor's gallery in Tribeca. I turned to ask Scarlet about that, but she had already gone.

Harriet then mentioned that following the art reception, attendees were free to hit the town, which I learned was code for pre-arranged dinners with vendors, and identified a number of restaurants offering conference discounts. I was exhausted just listening to the agenda. I took another swig of my coffee before noticing Nikki from Bespoke Adventures a few steps to my left, swigging down coffee as quickly as I was. She gave a nod of recognition.

"That was fun last night," I said.

"Too much fun," Nikki said, taking another sip of coffee as emphasis.

I laughed and asked, "Are the schedules always this crowded?"

"Yep," said Nikki. "Over the years, these kinds of conferences have gotten shorter, so they have to cram in as much as possible. With people's schedules the way they are, and the sheer number of events, it's harder to get buyers to give up too much of their time."

"Even if they're being wined and dined?"

Chapter Twelve

"Even if they're being wined and dined," she said, nodding. "With two full days of programming, this is one of the longer ones. Some are down to a day-and-a-half."

I realized I hadn't looked that closely at the schedule. "Tomorrow's the same as today?"

"Similar. Morning education sessions, followed by midday lunch and marketplace. They're offering tickets to a Broadway matinee in the afternoon. It's a limited number, but that's fine as a lot of the vendors will take off after the marketplace."

"Interesting," I said. "Obviously, I'm a total newbie to this whole scene. What show are they seeing?"

"I can't remember the name, but I think it's at the Palazzo Theatre."

The theater where Hastings worked. Not for the first time, I realized how far Maxine's tentacles reached in filling the conference with offerings from her friends—really, Tina's friends—be it Victor's gallery or Hastings' show, not to mention Scarlet's odd remark about protecting her investment. Maxine seemed to know how to rope people into things. Did that include Georg's hotel? Or was that a coincidence since she'd held her events at other recently renovated hotels in previous years?

I was about to respond to Nikki when Harriet started introducing the session. I indicated I would be taking a seat. Instead of joining me, Nikki nodded, picked up a pastry to go with her coffee, and backed out of the room. Interesting, but I guess she wasn't attending the conference for the education, just the marketplace. I took my seat and listened as Harriet introduced the panelists as legends in their fields who could provide an overview of the state of the luxury goods and services market. I smiled as this would be a piece of cake for Mona. But based on the look on her face as she walked out, she didn't seem happy about the other so-called legends on her panel: Georg and Victor. The latter I'd heard utter maybe a dozen words the whole time I'd known him. Or perhaps it was being called a "legend." It did connote, you know, "old."

I have to say, sitting together on the stage, they kind of looked like the industry's old guard. Don't tell them I called them that. Maybe legend was the better term, right? It didn't help that their panel would be followed by a crowd touted as some of the hottest young influencers in the industry.

I came back to Mona and wondered what she was thinking as Harriet started her questioning with Georg. Smooth move on Harriet's part, beginning with him, with the hotel offering up so many freebies to the conference. Or perhaps it was part of the contract. Who knew? Not me!

"Georg, why don't you tell us what decisions went into the redesign of The Françoise following its acquisition by Hotels du Jour?" Harriet said.

"Thank you, Harriet. As you know, while we have dozens of hotels throughout the European continent, this is Hotels du Jour's first foray into the American market. We couldn't be more pleased that we were able to start with a hotel with such a rich history. Good bones, as they say in the industry." Georg

Chapter Twelve

looked out at the audience and smiled. The man just oozed charm, I will give him that.

"Research we commissioned indicated an increasing importance—especially among the young affluent market—for hotels to reflect the unique characteristics of their destination. When dealing with a historic hotel with a rich narrative like The Françoise, it is important to honor that history while also bringing it up to the luxury standards of today," he continued. "I mean, we've all seen hotels that have done this badly... They will, of course, go unnamed." Again, with a smile. "But we've also seen the amazing results when historic buildings meld with modern sensibilities. A wonderful example can be found in some of the Paradors in Spain, especially the Parador de Leon..." He said the hotel name with a perfect Spanish accent. Of course.

"Victor, I believe you and your lovely wife stayed at that Parador recently, did you not?" Harriet asked.

All eyes turned to Victor, the man of very few words. "We did," he said, slowly. "Impeccable, both the art and interior design, and the way they coalesced the modern elements within the original monastery walls." I could see that if it was a topic that interested him, Victor did have a few things to say.

Georg nodded. "Exactly. This blending of authentic localities with a luxury experience for the traveler is more important than ever," he said, his passion for hotels quite evident. "Again, what our research tells us is that this is especially true for the young affluent market, who are looking for a more experiential form of travel, especially if it contains elements exclusive to them."

Georg turned to Mona. "I'm sure you've noticed this trend, Mona, in your travels for *Vogue* and now in your role as editor-in-chief at *Carmel Today*." The way Georg smiled at her made my knees buckle a bit again, and I was sitting in a chair. He really had a thing for her.

Mona seemed startled that Georg was bringing her into the conversation so quickly. "Yes, Georg, thank you for bringing that up," she said. "Although I think we are mistaken if we bring monolithic thinking to the young affluent demographic. Luxury as a concept is constantly changing, which is why it's important to include a variety of voices. That's something I've been striving for at *Carmel Today* by bringing on young and perhaps somewhat unconventional voices as writers and editors…"

Not to mention an ultra-hip travel columnist, I thought. I mean, she didn't say it, but she meant it, right? Or was I the unconventional voice? Either way, I was pleased as punch to get a call out.

"You know, you're right, Mona," Victor piped up, again proving he was happy to speak when the topic interested him. "The art world has been undergoing a similar trajectory. While we still see outrageous auction prices for works by those considered the masters of their day, we also find more and more collectors seeking young, diverse voices."

"Exactly," Mona said. "Exclusivity is not the end goal."

✦ Chapter Twelve ✦

"I never said that exclusivity was the end goal," Georg said, his voice straining just a little. "However, it is a part of the idea of luxury."

"But should it be? Who is the arbiter? Old white men like you?" Snap! Go, Mona!

"Of course not," Georg said. I was surprised to see his eyes showed more sadness than anger when he turned to look at her.

As Mona refused to meet his gaze, Harriet broke the tension by turning to Georg.

"Georg, why don't you tell us about some of the bespoke experiences your wonderful concierge team has put together here at The Françoise?"

Georg took a breath. The charming smile returned to his face as he began to speak about some of their "exclusive" offerings. I again noted how impressive Harriet was at managing the conversation, especially after all those years of living in Maxine's shadow. She was funny, extremely well-informed and well-spoken, and appeared to revel in her new role. It made me wonder why she had accepted taking a backseat to Maxine and doing her drudge work all these years. I looked over and saw her son Dmitri standing in what I'm assuming was her usual spot just off stage holding his clipboard. He had a smile on his face as well. Interesting.

When the session was over, they all received a hearty round of applause that seemed genuine. The discussion was definitely not boring. I made eye contact with Mona and gave her a thumbs-up. Although I could tell she was still unsettled after her interaction with Georg, she smiled and nodded. Harriet announced that the next session—featuring the young, and quite diverse based on the pictures in the program, influencer types—would follow a 15-minute break. As everyone left the stage, I tried to get close to Mona, but she was immediately mobbed by people asking her questions, so I backed off.

I walked back to the table with the coffee and pastries. There, I noticed a hotel employee with a long cart covered with a tablecloth replacing some of the empty trays of food with full ones before heading out of the ballroom. I decided to follow. I was still curious about all the hotel's nooks and crannies, especially those that might have helped Maxine get into the hotel without anybody seeing her. It also occurred to me that the cart was easily long enough to hide a body, even if I wasn't happy that the thought popped into my head.

With everyone seemingly occupied and zero interest in listening to influencers spout off about fashion-and-spa-product trends, I decided to take a more detailed snoop around the hotel. For my story, of course. I followed the path the employee took out of the ballroom and across the lobby area. There, I saw her disappear into a door near the front desk and the executive offices. Huh.

On the other side of the lobby near the entrance to the hotel, Renaldo was busy talking to some new guests, so I walked toward the back hallway where the guest elevators were located. I found a set of stairs at the end of the hall near the closed 5th Avenue entrance and decided to take them down to the basement level to see if I couldn't find the service entrance Leonora

Chapter Twelve

had mentioned. If my bearings were correct (always a crap shoot), I thought it might be the same area where I saw the employee with the cart disappear.

When I got to the bottom of the stairs, the door opened onto the same basement hallway I'd visited with Mona my first day at the hotel. I passed the elevators and then the Business of Luxury show office. The open door revealed an empty office, except for one sad-looking ambassador who had obviously been put in charge of handling the conference landline and appeared to be playing solitaire on her phone. I tiptoed past so she wouldn't see me and continued down the hall past a few more small meeting rooms on either side, and a corridor leading to a door marked "Private." Out of curiosity, I tried that door, and it was locked. Interesting.

Back in the main hall, a door at the end said "staff only." I tried the handle. The door opened, and I decided to check it out. As an ad hoc member of the Business of Luxury staff, "staff" meant me, right? I thought so or pretended I thought so, hoping that if I were caught it would be a good enough excuse. If there was one thing I had learned when covering crimes at the newspaper, playing oblivious worked like a charm when trying to sneak in somewhere you shouldn't be or asking questions that were a bit out of line. The "beleaguered airhead" persona I developed worked particularly well when trying to gain information. You know, something along the lines of: "Oh my god, my boss is going to kill me, but I think I made a mistake. Can you tell me [fill in the blank with an address, name, project, etc.]?"

That didn't mean I wanted to bring attention to myself, so I cracked the door open quietly and found an even more industrial-looking hallway with gray-toned walls and concrete floors. I tiptoed as stealthily as I could past a service elevator that, if my bearings were correct, was the one next to the front desk on the floor above. To my surprise, just after passing the elevator, it opened and Dmitri came rushing out. I ducked behind a door and watched as he strode quickly in the direction of the show office. Was The Françoise really allowing Business of Luxury staffers to use their service elevator? Maybe only Dmitri and Harriet since they needed to get back and forth to the lobby quickly, and there was often a wait at the guest elevators. Still, that did also allow them access to the non-public parts of the hotel.

Once the service entrance door closed behind Dmitri, I continued on. I found an employee cafeteria and locker room, laundry room, huge kitchen, and a nondescript-looking room with a bunch of computer monitors (maybe security computers? I didn't loiter too long to find out) before reaching a final door with a red "EXIT" sign above it.

That door led to a ramp up to a second door with a small window. I peeked through and saw what appeared to be a narrow alleyway and a wrought-iron gate where the building met the sidewalk. As I opened the door, I was immediately met with the noise of the street and the greater city beyond—and a squeak I hoped was not a rat. As I looked behind the doorway, I heard a voice from a small booth adjacent to the gate say, "I don't think you're supposed to be here."

CHAPTER THIRTEEN

I turned in the direction of the voice, letting the door slam behind me as I did, and found Officious Otto standing outside the booth at the gate. Oh my god, the man was everywhere! Although my heart was pounding in my chest, I did my best to stay cool and stick with my original plan of playing dumb. While I didn't have the blonde hair that might have helped pull off the airhead stereotype, I had perfected a California Valley Girl accent just for these types of situations.

"Dude! You are totally right!" I giggled (in case you are wondering, the giggle helps sell it). "So, like, I was in the Business of Luxury show office and went to find Candace, and I totally took a wrong turn."

I'm not sure Otto completely bought my story, but he nodded at the wall behind me. "That door stays locked at all times. Don't want to let the rats in." I wasn't sure if he was talking about the human or vermin variety.

"Oh, gee, totally no," I said, taking a bit of a jump even though I had made it this far on the trip without seeing anything resembling the vermin variety (thank god). "Is that an issue? Even at a swank hotel like this?"

"It's an issue everywhere in New York, including the park across the street and the building next door—" he said, nodding toward the wall adjacent to the service entrance. "But we are discreet in how we handle it," he said, pointing to some traps back in the corner.

Discretion is our middle name in everything, eh?

"Is the building next door the co-op?" I asked. "I am kind of turned around."

"No, the co-op is around the corner on the 5th Avenue side of the hotel. They're not bad. But the association that owns the mansion next door is very old school and not particularly conscientious about keeping their service entrance clean and refraining from the use of chemicals. It makes it difficult for us as we've been working toward achieving designation as a 'green' hotel."

"Oh, wow, that's so interesting," I said. "And totally something I can use in my story. Did Candace and Georg tell you I'm writing a story on the hotel for *Carmel Today*?"

I couldn't tell if he knew, but my mentioning it did seem to relax Otto. He nodded and cracked a semblance of a smile. "As you may imagine, it's not easy for a hundred-year-old building to be environmentally friendly," he said. "Especially as we also want to keep our designation as a historic landmark. We had to hide our solar panels on the roof. If you can see them from the street, the building is no longer considered historic."

"That's really cool," I said, still using my Valley Girl voice, but I did think it was cool and wanted him to know I was on his side. "I'll ask Candace to give me more information and quotes about it for my story."

"Glad I could be of service. In the meantime, you can't get back into the hotel that way," he said, pointing to the now-closed door with his usual officious-sounding voice. "Not without an employee keycard." He held up the card hanging around his neck as he backed onto the sidewalk and pointed toward The Françoise's awning on my left. "You'll have to come out to the street and go back through the main entrance."

"Of course," I said. "Man, I can be such a bonehead sometimes." I laughed, hoping he was buying my clueless act. "I'm from California, so this is confusing to me."

That brought me another crack of a smile. "Again, we're always happy to be of service," he said. "Come, I'll show you."

I followed Otto out to the sidewalk. As he escorted me to the front entrance, I took a peek at the building next door. They really did suction right up next to each other in this city. Built out of white stone, it was substantial. Smaller than The Françoise and more residential in style but with a similar feeling. I then remembered someone mentioning that it was built as a mansion for the family of the original owner. It was about the same height as Tina's brownstone—maybe five stories—but wider and more ornate.

Outside the entrance to The Françoise, we found Renaldo helping someone into a taxi.

"Ms. Powers. Welcome back. Have you been enjoying the city?"

"I found her in the service entrance," Otto said.

"A lovely bit of New York," I said. "Really, it should be on all the city tours."

Renaldo laughed as he nodded at Otto and opened the front door of the hotel for me. "We'll look into that."

I walked back into the lobby with my heart still pounding and immediately tried to blend in with the crowd in case Otto and Renaldo were still watching me. Thankfully, the education session had let out, and the lobby was filled with people milling about and chatting. I tried to figure out what to do next while still processing what I'd learned: It would be difficult for anyone to sneak into the hotel from the outside without an employee opening either the front door or that service entrance—an entrance Dmitri (and maybe Harriet?) had been granted at least some access to. That and there were possibly rats in the vicinity of the hotel.

While I pondered, I started looking for Mona. She was usually easy to find since she towered over everyone, but I didn't see her. I did find Harriet, standing with Victor near the concierge desk. Victor was on the phone while Harriet was looking over her clipboard with a large poster-sized cardboard box behind her.

"Hey, Harriet, have you seen Mona?" I asked.

Chapter Thirteen

Harriet looked up at me with a particularly harried look—yes, her nickname (except when she was being her super proficient self on stage) was Harried Harriet. "Huh? Oh, hello, Sam. No, I haven't seen her since her session, but she has marketplace appointments scheduled in the Gold Room, and they begin in five minutes."

"Oh, right. Is there anything I can do to help?"

The relief that came over her face was palpable. "Actually, there is. I can't find Dmitri or any of my ambassadors, and I need to get this signage down to Victor's gallery for our event there," she said, before muttering to herself, "and yet again, everything falls on me."

"I'm sorry?" I asked.

Harriet shook her head. "Nothing. Everyone's probably in the ballroom getting the lunch marketplace set up, but the van is already waiting outside. Could you go down with Victor to help set up?"

I decided not to mention seeing Dmitri or the bored ambassador downstairs since I wasn't supposed to be down there. And the truth was, I was hoping to talk to Mona. But I could tell Harriet was in a jam, and Mona would be busy for a couple of hours with the lunchtime appointments anyway. Mona had told me I was there to help wherever possible—and hey, this way I'd get to see some of the city—so I just said, "I'd be happy to help."

"Great," Harriet said, tapping Victor on the shoulder and pointing at me. "Sam can help."

Victor nodded, pointed at the parcel, and started walking toward the front door, still with his phone to his ear. Back to being a man of few words, I guess. I picked up the parcel and followed him. It should be an interesting journey.

We exited The Françoise and found a shiny black SUV waiting for us.

"This is the van Harriet mentioned?" I asked.

Victor nodded, continuing to hold his phone to his ear. Really, dude?

"Fancy van," I said under my breath (or so I thought).

"We also pick up the presenters and do other errands for the conference," I heard a voice with a slight French accent say. Soon, a large Black man with gray-flecked dreadlocks and a similarly flecked beard materialized from the driver's side of the SUV to help me wrangle the poster box into the back. "Maxine insisted we do that in style."

"You knew Maxine?" I asked, noting he was quite stylish himself in a black suit and skinny tie.

"I was her driver for 30 years," he said, smiling as we all got in, and he started pulling out into New York City traffic. The huge vehicle swung in and out of lanes with precision, sometimes coming within an inch of the cars on either side.

"Maxine had a personal driver? That's impressive," I said, scooting to the edge of my seat in the back so I could talk to the driver while Victor continued listening to whoever he was listening to on his phone. Maybe it was music. Or a podcast. Or just a ploy to avoid having to make small talk with me. "My name is Sam, by the way."

★ Chapter Thirteen ★

"I'm Omar. And I wasn't her personal driver, or a personal driver just for her, I should say," he said with a smile. "I run my own charter car service, and her company is one of my clients. But Maxine was my first client and a huge help when I was building my business. She mentioned it in her newsletter and referred me to everyone she knew on her list."

"I'm sure that's quite the list," I said.

"In its heyday, it was," Omar said. "Not so much recently."

An interesting statement on many levels. Not only that Maxine's influence was waning (not surprising with all the new "influencers" out there), but it was also the first benevolent act I had heard someone mention in connection with Maxine. I was intrigued.

"That was nice of her," I said. "Where did you meet?"

"On a Formula 1 track in Monaco," he said, oh so nonchalantly.

I laughed. "That's not something you hear very often."

"I worked with her first husband, Pierre, on his racing team and came with them when they moved to New York. By the time they broke up, I had fallen in love and started a family here. Maxine helped me stay." He got a wistful look in his eye as he dodged a taxicab that decided to suddenly brake inches in front of us to pick up a passenger. "But that was a long time ago."

"And yet you still have some pretty mad driving skills."

"This city either eats you up or makes you stronger," Omar said. "That's even true when it comes to driving."

I laughed again. "I can see why Maxine wanted to make sure you stayed in business."

Omar nodded, while also, thankfully, not taking his eyes off the road. "Thank you."

"I'm so sorry for your loss," I said, realizing just how many people's lives Maxine had touched.

"Thanks. It's still a bit of a shock."

"I just got to New York a few days ago and have heard so many stories about Maxine. I'm sorry I didn't get to meet her."

"She was a true New York character," Omar said. "In the best—and I suppose, worst—sense."

Not the first time I'd heard that so I asked, "In what way?"

Omar hesitated.

"Oh, please don't tell me discretion is your middle name, too," I said.

He laughed. "In this town, lack of discretion can kill your business—or worse."

Interesting choice of words. I looked over at Victor, still with the phone on his ear. He nodded, and I offered one in return.

"I understand," I said. "I just think it would be nice to know what happened to Maxine, don't you?"

"In what way?"

"Well, from what I heard, the last anyone saw of her was when she left The Françoise after the site tour. They claim she never came back to check into her suite, and yet she was found dead in the bathroom. That's weird, right?"

Victor glanced at me and appeared to frown as I said that.

★ Chapter Thirteen ★

"It is strange," Omar said, nodding.

"She never called you for a ride?"

"No. The last ride I booked for her was my pick up of Ms. Reynolds at JFK."

"You picked Mona up?"

"I did. I brought her to The Françoise, where she was supposed to meet Maxine, but Maxine wasn't there. That's when everyone started asking around."

"Huh."

Victor finally put his phone down. *Uh oh*, I thought, *am I in trouble for asking so many questions?* I'd always had a hard time with quiet people with frowny faces like Victor. What was he thinking?

"Omar, Walker is a one-way street so it'll be easier if you turn into the alley here and come around" was all he said.

"Will do, Vic."

I smiled at Victor. He nodded, so I guessed we were okay. We pulled down a narrow street filled with small buildings, again sitting side-by-side with no space between them. They all featured exterior fire escapes that created a mesmerizing geometric pattern.

"What neighborhood is this?" I asked Victor.

"Tribeca."

I nodded. In addition to the buildings being smaller in this neighborhood, it was a lot quieter than the Midtown area where Tina's brownstone and The Françoise were located. Very pleasant, actually. Almost like a small town in the middle of the big city. We pulled up in front of a white building with large windows and V&H Gallery stenciled on the front. Victor leaped out—pretty agile for an old guy,

I noted — while I helped Omar pull the cardboard box out of the back of the SUV and carry it into the gallery.

Once it was inside, Omar said, "It was nice meeting you, Sam. I have another call so I have to leave." He handed me his card. "If you need anything while you're in the city, you let me know, okay?"

"I will. Thanks for your help, Omar. It was nice meeting you as well."

As I put Omar's card in my bag, I noticed that Victor's phone had finally moved away from his ear — but before I could ask for help, he started tap tap tapping away on it. *Okay, I can figure this out*, I thought as I took the Business of Luxury poster out of the box and set it up to the side of the front entrance.

When Victor finally looked up, I asked, "Is this where it should go?" He nodded, so I decided to grab this brief moment when his gaze was averted from his phone. "Your gallery is beautiful. How long have you had it?"

"We opened this location in 1980," he said.

"You and Scarlet?"

"Me and Horatio." Victor pointed to a picture on the wall behind him of two young men in front of the building, which had construction scaffolding all over it. I could spot Victor, even if he had a massive head of very curly hair at the time and now was completely bald. Beside him was a huge man with long hair, a beard, and a paint-splattered set of overalls.

"That's Tina's Horatio?" I tried to picture the two of them together with Tina so tiny and this man kind of a giant.

Chapter Thirteen

"One and the same. I knew Horatio before Tina. We met at Pratt."

He was talking! Victor was talking! To me! I tried to keep him going. "You were an artist, too?"

"A bad one, yes. But I knew how to spot good art. Horatio was the best." He pointed to an enormous sculpture in a far corner of the gallery. "That's Horatio's."

"It's amazing."

"One of his first. One of his smaller ones, in fact. He has a few down on Wall Street in front of the big brokerage firms and another in front of a Midtown publishing house. From back in the days when companies commissioned interesting art, and this area was a ghost town filled with abandoned warehouses from its era as a mercantile center."

I looked outside at the vibrant series of galleries, cafés, and shops across the street and tried to picture what it might have looked like back then.

"Horatio found the building," Victor continued. "Above the gallery were the kinds of cavernous spaces where he could build his sculptures and a rooftop garden with a view of the Hudson River. I moved my gallery from Midtown to the first floor with the basement available for storage." He smiled wistfully. "In those days, getting people down here for shows was a challenge."

Those were by far the most words I'd heard the man utter. I again could see that if I happened upon a topic that interested him, he'd open up. I also realized how much history he'd seen in the city in his lifetime and wanted him to keep going.

"Do you still own the building?" I asked.

"Scarlet and I do, of course." He got a broad smile at the mention of his wife. "I was lucky enough to fall in love with a financial wizard who could aid us creative types."

I could use a Scarlet in my life, I realized.

"And Tina, too, of course."

"Tina owns this with you?"

"As Horatio's widow, yeah," Victor said. "After he died, we didn't need the studio space and turned the second and third floors into residential loft spaces. They bring in a nice income. Tina will always be taken care of."

Before I could ask more, I saw the most amazing sight behind him: a huge rectangular part of the floor opening up and a wrapped object starting to come up through it.

"What the heck is that?"

"Artwork elevator."

"Wow!"

Victor grinned. "We had it installed when we renovated the building. It used to go up into the second and third floors, too, as a way to bring Horatio's sculptures down. We sealed it off when the lofts were created, so it now just brings artwork to and from our basement storage area."

Another New York basement bestowing unseen wonders—but this one with a contraption à la Houdini. I then noticed caterers in the back setting up the bar and tables for the Business of Luxury reception. It looked like it was going to be a festive party amid all the art, which ranged from Horatio's huge

✦ Chapter Thirteen ✦

metal sculpture in the back to wall-sized oil portraits, and tiny black-and-white street photographs to a woman sitting inside a plexiglass box typing on what appeared to be carbon paper in a 1930s-era manual typewriter. Okay, that was interesting.

"I love the art in your gallery, Victor. It's so nice of you to allow the conference event to be held here," I said. "You must have been close to Maxine."

"I did not do this for Maxine," Victor snapped. "May she rest in peace and all that garbage. I do this for Tina, as did Scarlet."

"Scarlet?"

"Scarlet has been helping Maxine with her company—at Tina's request."

Interesting. Tiny Tina in action again.

"For some reason, Tina always had a soft spot for Maxine, and I have a soft spot for Tina because Horatio was my best friend," Victor continued, adding another slight smile. "The four of us had some wonderful times."

His face clouded. "Maxine changed everything. I always hated how she treated Tina. The constant leeching off her that only increased after Horatio's death."

What the hell did that mean? Before I could ask, I felt the buzz that meant a phone call was coming in. The moment I looked down to see it was from Mona, Victor disappeared. I'm sure expelling that many words—not to mention the sentiment behind them—was quite exhausting for the poor guy.

"Hi, Mona," I said, after clicking "accept."

"Sam, where are you?"

"I'm at Victor's gallery. Harriet had me help him with the event signage. Should I stay here until the event?" I asked, hoping I could explore more of the neighborhood.

"No. Get back to the hotel as soon as you can."

CHAPTER FOURTEEN

I was told the subway would be the fastest way back uptown, so I opened the GPS on my phone to find the station. After heading down the stairs, I used the electronic wallet on my phone to pay the fare like I did on the bus. I went through the turnstiles and then joined my fellow New Yorkers as we smashed inside the steel car that barreled its way through the city before dropping me a few blocks from The Françoise. Amazing.

Back at the hotel, I found Business of Luxury attendees getting onto the double-decker bus that would take them on a city tour culminating with the artist talk at Victor's gallery in Tribeca. Candace and Nikki waved from a window just inside the bus and pointed to a seat in the row behind them. I sadly shook my head to indicate I couldn't go with them and waved as the bus took off. Bummer.

When I walked through the revolving door and into the lobby, the first thing I saw was Dmitri being ushered into the executive offices by two detectives (badge and gun bulges under their suit jackets the dead giveaways). What was that all about? I pulled out my phone and called Mona. She picked up quickly.

"Are you back? I'm in my room. Come up as soon as you can."

I quickly made my way to the elevator, where I again found Leonora.

"Good afternoon, Ms. Powers."

"Please, again, call me Sam."

She smiled. "Sam. Would you like to go up to your room?"

"That would be lovely, Leonora. Thank you."

After I entered the elevator and she pushed the 7th floor without my having to ask, I decided to gather some intel using a little flattery. "How is it you are all so amazing at knowing everything about us?"

"I'm not sure what you mean, Ms. ... Sam."

"Well, just now, you remembered my room was on the 7th floor. And the other night when I got on the elevator, Otto knew my name just based on the room I came out of."

Leonora laughed. "Ah, yes. Well, our goal at The Françoise has always been to be as adept as possible at customizing the experience for our guests. We're given room lists at the beginning of our shifts each day that include their personal preferences."

"Personal preferences?"

Chapter Fourteen

"For instance, I will make sure to note that you very much prefer to be called by your first name," she said, smiling.

"Much appreciated."

"They also include things like desired room temperature or whether the guest is celebrating a special occasion, in which case a gift would be sent up to the room."

"Gift?"

"Chocolate-covered strawberries for an anniversary or a small cake for a birthday."

"How lovely!"

Leonora smiled. "Of course, not all of us are as adept as Otto at memorizing the names and room numbers so quickly."

"And preferences?"

"That depends on the department. Housekeeping has a much more detailed list. Of course, our concierge team often knows more than anybody."

I thought of the tall, impeccably dressed man who looked like the clerk in the *John Wick* movies standing behind the concierge desk when I first arrived. "I haven't had a chance to meet them."

"Well, they're all amazing. Between the four of them, they speak twelve languages and are well known within the industry for being able to make anything happen."

"Anything?"

"Tickets to the hottest show in town. Reservations at the most exclusive restaurants."

"Impressive."

"Two have achieved the Clef d'Or."

"And that is?"

"The highest certification a concierge can achieve." Her pride was apparent and sweet. "It's designated by the pin with the gold keys. All the luxury hotels have concierge desks, but our team is really special, and we're lucky to have them." She leaned over and whispered, "They even once helped someone skywrite a marriage proposal over Central Park on a day when the president was in town and the air space off limits. It was written up in a travel-industry magazine, so I'm not speaking out of turn."

"Yes, I've heard discretion is your middle name here at The Françoise. More than once," I said, wondering if their skill set included sneaking guests into the hotel without anyone seeing.

Leonora laughed. "It was our founder's motto. And the hotel's since it opened in 1920."

"I love how close you all are."

"Most of us have been here for decades. Some for generations. I know it can be a cliché, but we are a family. We are very lucky that the new owners kept us all on through the renovations and rebranding."

We reached my floor, and Leonora opened the gates. I wanted her to continue so stood in the doorway. "Have things changed much?"

Leonora shrugged. "A lot was behind the scenes, like new HVAC and technology systems. They did completely renovate the penthouse level since it had always been used as a private apartment."

"Oh, yeah, Candace showed me the rooftop bar."

Leonora nodded. "It's brought in a much younger clientele, which is great."

* Chapter Fourteen *

"I can imagine." I thought about how I'd seen Otto watching that elevator. "Tell me about Otto. I feel like he is kind of everywhere."

"That's his job," Leonora said, brushing the question off with a shrug. "He rotates around filling in for almost every position here at the hotel."

"He must see everything that goes on."

"That might be true. I obviously only see this little sliver." Leonora pointed to the small booth.

"A sliver that everyone who stays here uses—and is being well watched," I said, pointing to the security camera in the back corner of the elevator.

"I suppose that's true," Leonora said, getting more nervous. "I don't think about it."

"Leonora, do you know if the police reviewed the security footage from the two nights before Maxine died?"

She got even more rattled. "I'm sorry?"

"I just saw the police in the lobby, so I'm wondering if anyone ever reviewed the footage to see how Maxine got into the hotel without anybody seeing her."

Leonora looked down.

"Discretion still your middle name, Leonora? Even when someone dies?"

"Please..." she said with her head still facing down.

I felt terrible for how uncomfortable I was making her so backed into the hall. "Okay, I get it. Thank you, Leonora. We'll talk later."

A visibly relieved Leonora closed the elevator gates. "Have a nice evening, Ms. Powers."

163

Ouch. Back to the formality. "You as well," I said as the doors closed. I turned to walk down the hall, where I again found Mona already waiting outside.

"Sam, thank god you're here," Mona said.

"What's going on? I saw some detectives talking to Dmitri. Has something changed?"

"You could say that."

"What?"

"Come in, come in," she said. I walked into Mona's suite and noticed a bouquet of flowers sitting on the coffee table. I couldn't quite read the writing, but the name "Georg Keller" was stenciled across the top of the card in black ink.

Before I could ask about the flowers, Mona continued, "I was with Dmitri and Harriet in the Gold Room when the detectives arrived. They told us that some preliminary lab results came back and the glass found next to Maxine tested positive for bromethalin."

I thought back to the ketamine vial and the consensus that Maxine had been regularly taking it. "Is that a fancy word for ketamine?"

"No. They found that, too, but the vial was still full, and they said the tox screen will take a while. This is something else, found in the residue of her glass. Something toxic, meaning whoever helped her sneak back into the hotel—after her bender or visit to a ketamine clinic or wherever she went—poisoned it. Not enough to kill her, but it incapacitated her to the point that she drowned."

"Oh my god," I said. "But why would they be talking to Dmitri?" I thought back to seeing him use the service elevator.

★ Chapter Fourteen ★

"They're talking to everyone who was on site that day. They already talked to me and to Harriet. All the employees who were here during the time in question have been interviewed again as well."

So that's why Leonora was so spooked. "I can't imagine they're saying much," I said. "Discretion being their middle name and all."

Mona laughed. "Yes. We'll see how far that goes. Georg has instructed them to cooperate. Discreetly, of course."

"Of course. I'm guessing he's as in the dark as we are since he arrived just before we found the body."

"Yes. 'Just flew in from Gstaad,' and all," Mona said, mimicking his accent.

I took a moment before diving in: "Okay, I'm sorry, but I have to know. What is the deal with Georg?"

"The deal?"

"Come on. It's been obvious since the first time I saw you together that there was something between you two. You've lied to me at least twice that I know of on this trip and are constantly talking in code with your friends," I said before pointing at the flowers. "And I can't help but notice that the man just sent you flowers."

Mona looked away, so I continued: "Mona, I've known you my whole life. My mom was your babysitter. You're friggin' dating my Uncle Henry. I thought I knew you, but I'm starting to feel like I don't know you at all."

Mona turned back to me, surprised. She put a reassuring hand on my arm. "Oh, Sam, dear. I don't want you to feel like that."

165

"Then tell me: Were you and Georg a thing?"

Mona looked at me, and then finally said. "In a form, yes, I suppose that's accurate."

"In a form? Mona, I see your reaction to the man."

She sighed and sat down on the couch. "I did bring you here to get your reactions, didn't I?" I sat in the chair across from her. "Okay, yes," she continued. "Georg and I were once in love. A long time ago, and as much as he's capable of the emotion."

"Meaning?"

"Meaning Georg has always been very driven. We met a couple years after I arrived in New York. My goodness, that's almost 40 years ago now. Hard for me to believe." She sighed again, and I gave her a reassuring smile. "I had gotten my dream job as an assistant editor at *Vogue*. He was a group sales manager at The Plaza. We had a photo shoot at his hotel." Mona got a sly smile. "He was, of course, gorgeous."

"Still is."

Mona nodded a tad ruefully. "Still is. And intelligent and driven. He comes from a long line of hospitality professionals. When I met him, he had just finished hotel management school in Switzerland. Spoke four languages."

Ah, his accent made sense now. "Very continental."

"Especially for a young woman from Central California," she said. "I will admit I loved the attention. He's quite seductive, you know."

"You don't need to tell me," I said. "I've met the man."

Mona smiled. "Although I acted sophisticated, I was quite young and naïve. Growing up in Monterey

* Chapter Fourteen *

with people like your mother as role models, I thought everyone only had people's best interests at heart."

"Mom always did, didn't she?"

"Yes, she did." Mona squeezed my hand before continuing. "After a while, I learned that beneath Georg's very attractive…"

"And very charming."

"…and very charming exterior, he was… I don't know… ruthless?"

Ruthless? What an odd word to use. "In what way?"

"In that Georg sees people as commodities. A means to an end." She got a wistful look. "We were together almost a year and had a lot of fun. The ultimate young New York power couple: parties at *Vogue*, The Plaza, Tina's…"

Mona paused, and I thought of all the young professional types I'd seen at the rooftop bar.

"And then he moved on," she continued. "I wasn't blind. I saw it coming."

A light bulb went off. "Maxine?"

Mona looked surprised. "How'd you know?"

I shrugged. "Just putting the pieces together."

She nodded. "Maxine had just started her own public relations agency. She managed to get a lot of press for a new boutique hotel where Georg had been named director of sales and marketing. Their affair was short-lived, but ultimately it changed everyone's lives."

"How so?"

"Well, we broke up. Obviously."

"And yet you and Maxine stayed friends?"

Mona rolled her eyes and shrugged. "I would call us friendly, not friends. We were in the same industry. And we had the Tina connection, of course."

I nodded as if I understood, but I'm not sure I did. "And Georg?"

"Georg ran off to Paris. Took a job as the general manager at a new hotel owned by Desiree's family. Naturally, he set his sights on Desiree. After Maxine learned they were an item, she announced that she was pregnant."

"Pregnant? Wow. What happened?"

"I don't know the particulars, but an arrangement was made... Tina was involved."

Tina again, I thought. All roads led to Tina. And then it clicked. "Wait a minute... Hastings?"

Mona nodded. "Hastings. Tina and Horatio sent Maxine off to stay with an artist friend of theirs who lived in Monte Carlo. After Hastings was born, Maxine stayed in Europe. Tina brought the baby back to New York and adopted him."

"So... the story of Hastings' parents dying in a car crash?"

"Like all good lies, it was built on some truth. Tina's sister and brother-in-law did die in a car crash but a good five years earlier. Still, it worked. Tina and Horatio brought up Hastings. Georg married Desiree and started managing some of the top hotels in Europe. Maxine went back to being... well... Maxine. She married a French race car driver she met in Monte Carlo, returned to New York, and Maxine Martinique was born. The marriage didn't last, but the persona did.

Chapter Fourteen

The newsletter and the conference followed. Those became her babies, I suppose."

"And no one ever said anything?"

"Not that I know of."

"Hastings has no idea?"

"I've always wondered but never asked."

"When I talked to him about Maxine, he didn't make it seem like they were particularly close."

"I'm sure Maxine did that on purpose, but the truth is I don't think she was particularly close to anyone. All her marriages were short-lived, and she kept people at a distance."

"Even Harriet?"

Mona thought for a moment before nodding. "Even Harriet. They each filled a need the other craved—Maxine offered Harriet excitement. In return, Harriet kept things running for Maxine."

"Symbiotic?" I offered.

"Transactional." Mona sighed again. "It has been my experience, Samantha, that people who constantly strive for fame and fortune or whatever it was Maxine was looking for only see people for what they can bring them. In a way, she and Georg had that in common."

"Except that at the time of their affair, neither had the kind of clout the other craved, huh?"

"I suppose that's true," Mona said. "Clout. It's such a silly word, isn't it? Did you know that it also means to hit or beat someone?"

"I actually did know that."

"Fits, I suppose. So many people are beaten up in the name of… what? Power? Prestige? Status?"

Mona looked outside at the city and sighed. "It's all so ephemeral, Sam, isn't it? I'll admit that when I was younger, I craved that excitement. That's why I moved here. Bright lights, big city, as they say." She sighed again and looked at me. "But what I learned after all my years of covering those who had reached the pinnacle of fame and fortune is that very few of them are happy."

"Thank god I'm mediocre then, eh?" I said, trying to lighten the mood.

Mona laughed, touched my knee, and looked me straight in the eye. "You'll never be mediocre, my dear."

But will I be happy? I wondered. *Or at least content?* Before I could ponder any further, Mona asked the question that had been on my mind. "But who would want to hurt Maxine? Especially now?"

Based on what I'd heard about the woman, the answer to the first question was: a lot of people. The bigger question was why now—and how did they pull it off?

CHAPTER FIFTEEN

Rat poison. Bromethalin is a chemical found in rat poison. I learned that when I went back to my room, laid down on the bed (oh god, that felt good), and texted Roger to ask if he'd ever heard of it. A moment later, he called.

"Are you kidding me?"

"About what?"

"We just had a session on poisons, and it came up."

"No way!" That wasn't my California Valley Girl act. I just talk like that sometimes.

"Way!" Was he mocking me? "As it happens, rat poison is particularly popular here in New York, mostly because a lot of people happen to have it on hand. Bromethalin is found in a powdered form of rat poison that's considered less toxic, but a dusting can still do some real damage. Doesn't usually kill a grown person, but combined…"

"With vodka and maybe even ketamine…"

"Could cause paralysis."

"Yikes."

"Where did you find out about the bromethalin?"

"Mona. The cops talked to her after they found residue in Maxine's martini glass. I guess they are going to talk to me soon as well since I was one of the people that found the body. Any tips?"

"You did pretty well when I first interviewed you." His voice had a funny sound to it.

"Detective Kai, are you flirting with me?"

"God, I hope so."

"Have you been drinking?"

"Maybe a little. After the poison session, some of us decided we needed a break, so we're at the hotel bar."

"What about Chief Akiona?"

"He left this morning. His daughter was starting to go into labor."

"And you?"

"My flight is tomorrow morning, but I still have to give his report and attend the final reception."

"Wait. So, you are free? And you didn't call?" I'm not going to lie. My ego was a little bruised.

After a beat, he said, "I assumed you were busy with the conference and the dead lady."

"Maxine. She has a name." I said that snippier than I should have, but come on, man.

"You mean you are free?"

"At this particular moment, yes, although it sounds like the detectives will be making their way to me soon."

"We haven't had a lot of luck, have we?"

* Chapter Fifteen *

"Or I guess, I don't know, desire..." Okay, I said it. I'm not sure if it was the lack of sleep or the ride I just took through the city or all the drama surrounding Maxine's death, but it popped out of my mouth before I could really think it through.

"What does that mean?" Roger said, the sexy drunk voice fading quickly. I could tell he was moving away from the bar to talk to me as the background noise level also dropped.

"Just... I mean, Roger, I've been here for three days now. Three tantalizing days where I've been just a couple miles away, and you haven't really seemed all that eager to see me."

"Are you kidding, Sam? I'm here in this godforsaken place for work. With my boss. At the last minute, you tell me you're coming, but all the way across town and entangled with a conference and a missing lady and then a dead body. Sometimes two miles is more than two miles..."

Let me preface this by saying that I'm not proud of this moment, but my frustration had reached a breaking point. With everything. And did I mention I hadn't been getting any sleep? "And when is two miles not two miles?" I asked.

"What are you talking about?"

"I don't know. You're in Hawaii. I'm in California. Now even when we're in the same city, we can't seem to make it work."

Silence. And then in the saddest tone possible, making my heart break just a little, he said, "You don't think this is working?"

Oh god. I didn't mean it like that. "No, I don't mean that, I mean..."

"No, I hear you, Sam." The tone became a lot more clipped. The military training kicking in, I suppose. "I guess I was misguided enough to think we were doing a pretty good job at making it work, even with the obstacles thrown in our way."

"We are...." I said, trying to backtrack.

"We are quite obviously not, based on what you just said."

"But..."

"But nothing. Here's the thing, Sam. I feel like I have been trying to make it work. I flew out to see you for your birthday. I flew out to see you when you moved out of your old apartment..."

And there it was. Lizzy was right. He was doing all the work, and instead of appreciating that or giving back, I just kept expecting more. But it wasn't like I had the type of bank account that would let me fly to Maui all the time or had a sister who let me use her flight benefits the way his did (and, yes, I even sounded whiny in my own mind).

Before I could answer with any of that or ponder what the correct response should be, he continued: "I even lied to my boss and skipped out of a session to meet you in Central Park yesterday..."

Okay, that I didn't know.

"...but just because I didn't stop everything I was doing to run across town to see you the moment you landed or now, not ten minutes after our session ended, I'm the one not making it work?"

★ Chapter Fifteen ★

"No," I said, quieter. This was the first time I'd heard him get upset. And he wasn't wrong. My frustration with life—not just here in New York, where I seemed to keep running into brick walls, but also back in Carmel with the leaky house and the sick father and feeling trapped—was spilling over to one of the best things in my life: Roger. I wasn't sure what to say and was still formulating a response while trying not to cry when a knock came at the door. "Just a second, there's someone at the door."

"Of course there is."

His tone made my heart ache. As I desperately pondered what I could say or do to make it all better, I opened the door and found myself face-to-face with one of New York's finest (as they say). I recognized him as the younger of the two detectives I had seen down in the lobby. Ah fuck.

"Hello, Ms. Powers."

I held my index finger up and pointed to my phone to indicate I needed a moment.

"Excuse me, Detective Kai," I said to Roger. "I have a Detective..."

"Anastos," the detective said.

"...Detective Anastos here to see me. Let's talk again soon." Before Roger could say anything more, I pushed "end call" and turned to the detective. "That's my... friend..." I wasn't sure I could say boyfriend at this point. "...Detective Roger Kai of the Maui police department. He's over at the Midtown Hotel for the forensics convention. I take it you're not attending?"

That got me a slight smile. "I am not," Anastos said, "and I apologize for the interruption, but if you don't mind, we have a few more questions regarding the death of Maxine Martinique."

"Happy to oblige." I opened the door wider to indicate he could enter.

"Actually, we are set up downstairs in the general manager's office."

"Lead the way then."

I closed the door and followed Detective Anastos down the hall to the elevator, where Otto was waiting instead of Leonora. I nodded at Otto, and he nodded back—a moment where I appreciated their famous reputation for discretion.

Once downstairs, I followed Anastos through the lobby and over to the executive offices behind the front desk, just like I'd seen them do with Dmitri. I entered the same office where they'd kept us after we found the body and where I'd found Mona talking to Georg the day before. I flashed back to Candace saying it was their general manager's office and that Georg was just using it while he was in town. I noted photos of a jovial-looking man with his family, clearly not Georg and Desiree, sitting on the desk alongside a computer monitor. Seeing the computer made me wonder if the detectives had reviewed any of the security tapes on that monitor.

It was not Georg or the man in the photos sitting behind the desk. Instead, a detective, if the ill-fitting suit and shoulder holster were any indication (they were), stood up when I entered and pointed to the chair across the desk. Detective Anastos sat in the chair next to me. It was interesting the way they had penned me in. I wondered if they did this with everyone.

Chapter Fifteen

"Hello, Ms. Powers, I'm Detective Garcia," the older man said, putting his hand out to shake.

Ah, Detective Garcia, I thought, remembering it as the name of the detective Mona said had completely discounted the idea that Maxine's death was anything other than an accidental drowning. *A little rat poison in a martini glass sure changes things, doesn't it, Detective Garcia?*

"It's nice to meet you," Detective Garcia continued.

"And you, Detective Garcia."

"I'll get right to it. As I'm sure you've heard, we've had a development."

"Oh?" Yes, I was back to playing dumb. It was doing me well, so I figured why not see what cards they had up their sleeves. That and I was still unnerved after my conversation with Roger and here I was faced with another detective, another friggin' detective. But I digress.

"An unfamiliar element was found in an item alongside the deceased."

"Oh? And that was?"

"Something that might have caused enough drowsiness for her to drown."

"As if a liter of vodka wouldn't do that already," Detective Anastos added.

Are you the bad cop, Anastos? I thought. TV stereotypes aside, what his comment told me was that they didn't really care what caused Maxine to slip into that water. Just another New York lush sinks to her death in a luxury hotel. My guess was that some higher-up was making them go through the motions to tie things up as quickly as possible, and the rat poison threw a wrench into that plan. I offered a wry smile.

"Why are you smiling?"

"I should tell you that my father was the chief of police in Carmel, California, and my uncle teaches criminal law at the Monterey School of Law," I said, dropping the airhead act just a bit.

Detective Garcia smiled. "So you know the drill, as it were."

"I do. And I have to say I thought something was wonky right off the bat and found it interesting you didn't feel the need to do more investigating in the first place," I said. "I also know that you probably don't use the word wonky in your reports."

That got a smile from both of them.

"We're here now, Ms. Powers," Detective Garcia said. "Why don't you expound on what you found so ... wonky?"

I went over the timeline again: Mona's call that Maxine had disappeared, my flight out, Mona and I running into Georg when he arrived at the hotel, him taking us up to the room where we found her body along with the martini glass with two olives, an empty bottle of Laporte vodka, and a vial of ketamine.

"Speaking of which, was there ketamine in her system?" I asked.

"We don't have the tox screen back yet," Detective Garcia said.

"Tell us again about this call from Mona Reynolds," Detective Anastos said.

"I'm not sure what you mean."

"Why would she ask you to come to New York?"

Chapter Fifteen

"Uh, because Maxine was missing."

"And..."

"And, she thought that, based on my background—I was also a crime reporter—I might be able to help. The police certainly weren't doing anything at that point."

I gave them my best impression of a Mona glare that said I was very much not impressed with their police work all around.

"Is that all?"

"I guess she also thought I could help with the conference. Mona was speaking at Maxine's conference, as she did every year, and was scheduled to meet with her the day she disappeared."

I left out the part about the illegitimate child Maxine had via an affair with Georg that caused his breakup from Mona. As Detective Garcia wrote a few notes on his legal pad, I tried to look at the computer screen to the side of him.

"Can you access the security tapes on that?" I said, pointing to the monitor.

"Why do you ask?"

"The thing I could never figure out—the wonkiness I referenced—is how Maxine got back into the hotel without anybody seeing her. I mean, the woman disappears and then turns up dead in a bathtub. A death you've finally determined might be suspicious. So how did that happen? Did you find her key card on her? The front desk said it was never used to activate her door."

"I don't think you need to trouble yourself with that," Detective Anastos said. I swear if he added the word "missie" I was going to slug him.

"We'll find out what happened," Detective Garcia added with a smug smile. "Leave it to us."

CHAPTER SIXTEEN

Leave it to us. Now that pissed me off. On the other hand, maybe they were right. *Maybe it is time to leave things to the professionals,* I thought. *Mona brought you in to raise the questions. You've done that, and the police are now looking into what happened to Maxine. Why should you care so much about someone you've never met—especially someone who was responsible for breaking Mona's heart and bringing so much pain to so many people?*

After the police said I could go, I walked back into the lobby, wondering what my next move should be. I looked at the time: 5:30 p.m. It was too late to go down to the event at Victor's gallery. After that, everybody would be going their separate ways on outings, none of which I was invited to. I knew Mona was going to dinner with some of her former *Vogue* colleagues. And I'd just had a fight with Roger, who was busy with his stupid conference anyway. What was a girl in a big city like New York to do?

I noticed that the entrance to the lounge had opened, so I wandered in and took a seat at the bar, watching as a series of young professional types made their way over to the elevator that took them to the rooftop bar. A hotel employee I hadn't met checked their IDs before allowing them access. I guess the rooftop bar was back in business after serving as the ad hoc hospitality suite for the conference all day.

"Hello, Ms. Powers," Hipster Julio said, walking over to my end of the bar. "Would you care for a drink? Perhaps another Françoise martini?"

"I would love one," I said. I mean, what the hell, right? As he poured the Laporte vodka into the shaker, something about seeing the bottle together with the elevator to the rooftop bar, started tickling something in my brain. As did the question of how even a trace of rat poison could end up in a hotel that prided itself on the fact it didn't use any chemicals.

I took a tiny sip of the industrial-strength liquid Julio placed in front of me and pondered my next step. As if the universe was answering my question, I got a text from an unknown number.

"Hey, Sam, this is Hastings. Tina gave me your number. We had a pair of house seats open up for the show tonight. Want to come?"

Before I could respond, a second text came in. "Winston will be your date."

I pondered. I mean, nobody needed me for anything, and my job was to cover the city after all. What

Chapter Sixteen

screams New York more than attending a Broadway show with a distinguished British actor?

"I would love to," I texted back.

"Great! Winston said he will meet you at the upstairs bar at Sardi's at 6:30."

I ran up to my room, wondering what the hell one wore to a Broadway show. I decided to throw on the outfit Mona picked out for me for the reception the night before and grabbed a jacket to go with it before jumping in a cab. Naturally, the cab decided to take a route that passed directly by the Midtown Hotel, the sign seemingly mocking me as we passed. *Roger is probably in there giving his speech,* I thought, still wondering how I'd managed to fuck things up so royally. Would we talk it out later, or was this when we just kind of let things peter out? We still lived more than 2,000 miles apart. What were the chances we could make it work?

When the cab got a few blocks away from 44th Street, not moving in bumper-to-bumper traffic, I told the driver he could pull over, and I would walk the rest of the way. It seemed silly for either of us to just sit there. I got out and started walking through the scrum of people where 7th Avenue and Broadway converged. Between the lights and the sounds and the sheer crush of humanity and cars and huge billboards filled with flashing lights, it was quite a sight. One I wanted desperately to escape.

When I made it to 44th, I turned right, and about a half block down found the red awning that said "Sardi's" on a block filled with other restaurants and at least three or four Broadway theaters. I had to admit it was kind of exciting, and I felt a buzz as I entered. Similar to how I felt walking into The Françoise the first time, my immediate reaction was that I'd gone back in time. Old school waitstaff in red jackets and black pants milled about a large dining room beyond the host stand and a small bar to my left. Since the text indicated I should meet Winston in the upstairs bar, I headed up the staircase to my right. There, I spotted him sitting at a high-top table next to a large window overlooking the street.

"You made it out of the madness," Winston said as I arrived at the table.

"Madness is right," I said. "I had to walk the last few blocks and in these stupid heels!"

He laughed. "I would say I don't know the experience except that I once starred in *La Cage Aux Folles*..." He took a sip of his martini. "In Del Rey Beach, Florida, of all places."

"Ah, the glamorous life of an actor. Eh, Winston?"

"You said it. I won't go into the voice work I did for corporate sexual harassment seminars." Winston laughed. "Please, Samantha, sit down, and I'll see if Vincent can get you a drink. They make an excellent martini here."

"Do they have a signature martini? I feel like everybody has their own style," I said.

"I suppose that's true," Winston said, as one of the red-jacket-clad bartenders appeared at our table. "Hello, Vincent. Ms. Powers would like a martini. Is there a signature Sardi's martini?"

Chapter Sixteen

"It's more that we know how to make a proper martini," Vincent said, dripping with disdain—or pride. Either way, it was impressive.

"Would you be so kind as to make a proper martini for Samantha?"

Vincent nodded and turned to me. "Do you have a spirit preference?"

"Spirit preference?"

"A particular brand of London Dry gin?"

I thought about Maxine's famous (or infamous) form of martini. "Not vodka?"

"A classic martini uses gin. Some people are not fond of the botanicals and prefer the neutrality of vodka."

"Some people don't even want the vermouth," Winston said.

"Basically, they just want a shot of vodka and some olives in a fancy glass," Vincent added, the two of them sharing a contemptuous chuckle.

"Well, if I'm to have a proper martini, it sounds like I need the proper spirit," I said, "with whatever London Dry gin you recommend, Vincent."

"Excellent choice," Vincent said, nodding before heading back to the bar. I looked around at some of the caricatures of actors lining the walls on both floors. "Will I find you on the wall?"

Winston rolled his eyes. "You will, although it's dated as it's from a show I did 30 years ago. See if you can find it."

I looked around at the hundreds of caricatures and then back at him. "That might take me a while."

"Okay, fine, it's in the hall leading to the restrooms, and yes you may make whatever quip you'd like about my career going into the toilet."

I laughed and walked down the hall, finding his picture along the way. Even though his currently silver hair was then dark brown, his aquiline nose and impish smile gave him away. That and if I wasn't mistaken (and I don't think I was), he was wearing the same cravat he had on at the reception. While I was in the vicinity, I figured I might as well use the bathroom and was surprised to find an attendant. A bathroom attendant! I mean, I'd heard about them, but it wasn't something I had come across in California. I had not brought my purse from the table and felt a stab of guilt in not adding to the attendant's tip jar. I mumbled something about coming back with cash and made my way back to the table with Winston.

"Well?" he asked.

"So debonair."

Winston laughed. "You're sweet." He pointed to some food on the table, along with my martini, which I noticed had a lemon twist as the garnish. "I hope you don't mind that I ordered some appetizers."

"I'm happy you did. I haven't eaten anything since breakfast."

"And these martinis can be lethal. No pun intended."

I laughed but also felt another ping as Winston's comment triggered something in my brain about Maxine's martini. I decided to probe his knowledge of the darn things.

"I have to admit they all kind of taste the same to me," I said, taking a sip and noting the gin did

Chapter Sixteen

have more of an herbal flavor than the vodka. "I know Maxine had a very special order."

"Dry, dirty Bonheur vodka martini up with three olives, eat one before you take a sip to establish a base."

"Wow, you definitely have that down."

He sighed. "You only had to watch Maxine berate one bartender before you learned the recipe." He got quiet for a moment, and then picked up his glass. "I'd like to offer a toast to a dear departed friend."

"To Maxine," we toasted, even if I'd never met the woman.

"I'm not sure if I should say this, but you seem to be a bit more broken up about her death than some of the others," I said.

"Except Tina," he said.

"Yes, except Tina."

"Well, my dear, as you may have guessed, I enjoy a little drama now and then. Maxine always brought the drama."

"How long have you been in New York?"

Winston sighed. "Going on 50 years now. *Quel horror!*"

"What brought you here?"

"The theater, of course. I came with a Royal Shakespeare group doing a series of plays at the Public and never left."

"Fell in love with the city?"

"Fell in love *in* the city would be more accurate," Winston said wistfully and then paused. "Matthieu passed away ten years ago."

"I'm so sorry. Was he an actor as well?"

"Actor, singer, dancer. Triple threat. He was amazing. Did a lot of musical theater." Winston laid a soft hand on the caricature above our table of a dashing man in a black bow tie and top hat similar to Renaldo's getup at The Françoise. "Matthieu, meet Sam. Sam, Matthieu."

My heart broke. "Nice to meet you, Matthieu," I said to the picture. "He's very handsome," I whispered to Winston.

"I know," he said with a gleam in his eye. "And just as beautiful inside."

I felt a pang as I thought about my fight with Roger and decided to move on before I started tearing up again. "Is that how you met Tina?"

"It is! Matthieu and Tina danced together in one of their first shows in the city. They became fast friends, together with Horatio and Victor, and then Scarlet. After we met, they became our family, along with the greater theater community here in New York. Matthieu helped Tina with the studio, and I went from playing Noel Coward aristocrats to old butlers. Such is the way of life, I suppose."

I loved hearing how they all helped each other out and realized my feelings of having life heaped on me and me alone were perhaps more self-imposed than I wanted to admit. What had Tina told me? Ask for help. And make it a party.

Before I could ponder more, Winston said, "If we want to make the curtain, we should start heading out. The theater is right across the street, but as you learned on your way here, getting past the scrum of

★ Chapter Sixteen ★

humanity in this area requires some time, and I'm not quite as nimble on my feet as I used to be."

I went to try to pay, but Winston waved me off. "It's already been taken care of." He stood and crooked his arm. "Are you ready, m'lady?"

"Most ready, Sir Winston." Check it out, I got to use my nickname for him in real life! I got a big smile in return, and the two of us headed down the stairs and across the street, slipping between people and cabs and cars and trucks and bikes before entering the lobby of the theater about halfway down the block. We took our programs and walked down to the orchestra level, passing people in attire that ranged from very dressy to quite casual, which meant I didn't really have to wear these darn heels.

"Fancy," I said as we reached our seats about seven rows back from the stage.

"The fanciest," Winston said. "These are the house seats or producers' seats. They keep them set aside in case a VIP wants them. Lucky for us, no one did this evening."

"So, if we didn't take them, they would just sit empty?"

"If no one takes them, they release them at a steep discount to the TKTS booth that the Broadway Theater League runs or to people who come to the box office looking for last-minute rush tickets."

Wow. There was so much about this world—and world within a world—that I didn't know. "It was nice of Hastings to think of us," I said. "These are amazing seats."

"He's a good kid, he is."

"You've watched him grow up."

"I have. We all have."

"Especially with his parents not around..." I said, probing a bit.

"As far as he knows, yes," Winston said with a sharp look in my direction. "And that's how it will stay."

Before I could respond, the music began to play, and the lights began to dim. Soon, I was mesmerized by the spectacle before me. And what a spectacle! Talented singers belting out songs, dancers moving in ways I didn't think possible, and sets flying in and out from above and below—and even rotating.

"That was amazing," I said, a little over an hour later when the curtain came down at intermission following what only can be described as a blockbuster number.

"Quite the spectacle," Winston said. "The leads just killed." He looked at me. "Sorry, I forgot... again."

"Hey, we share the inappropriate humor gene, remember?"

"That's right. Another reason we already love you, Samantha." Winston gave my shoulder a hug as we stayed in our seats while others bustled about or ran to the bathrooms.

"I realize I haven't asked you what you learned from the detectives," he continued. "Harriet told us they came back to talk to everybody at the hotel. Do they really think she was murdered? I have to admit I just assumed it was natural causes."

"I guess there was a trace of bromethalin found in her glass. Not enough to kill her but enough to

Chapter Sixteen

make her super drowsy, especially combined with the vodka."

"Rat poison?" Winston said. "How odd, although it is somewhat of a ubiquitous presence in the city."

Interesting that he knew the chemical. Although as he said, it was kind of everywhere, including in a box in Tina's kitchen, as I recalled.

"It would be a miracle if we all haven't ingested a little," Winston continued.

That was an interesting thought. What if it was all accidental after all? I wondered. Before I could deliberate too long, the second act began, and I was again pulled into the spectacle of a Broadway musical. Before I knew it, the show was over, and everyone was on their feet as the cast members came out for a bow and a final sing-a-long with the audience. As I experienced the symbiotic buzz that came from the artistry I'd just witnessed, I felt Winston pulling me toward the stage.

"Come on, let's go visit Hastings. And Sarah."

"Sarah?"

"The woman who played the grandmother is a friend of ours."

Of course she is, I thought. Before I knew it, Winston led me to a door to the right of the stage. An usher stood in front of the door, but Winston introduced himself and told him we were there to see Hastings and Sarah. The usher nodded and opened it for us. Really, that's all it took? Or was it like The Françoise, and they had memorized the names of those allowed to enter? Either way, the magical evening continued as I followed Winston through the door and up a set of stairs that led to the stage. The stage!! I looked at the back of the curtain that now separated us from the seats as Winston saw a woman at the back of the hall and walked quickly over to see her.

"Sarah, my dear, you were glorious, as always," Winston said, embracing her in a hug.

While they were catching up, I heard a "psst" and found Hastings standing a few feet behind me next to a huge panel filled with all sorts of switches and lights.

"Hey there," he said with a smile that lit up his face.

"Hey there yourself," I said, smiling despite myself. God, he was good-looking. Aesthetically speaking, of course. "Thank you for the tickets. That was so fun!"

"I'm glad you got to come and experience the magic of the theater."

"It is magical. You're all so magical. Really."

Between the joy of the show and the martinis I seemed to be living on in the city, I was on a bit of a high.

"How did you get the castle to disappear like that at the end?"

"Want to see?"

"I'd love to."

"Go stand on that blue mark in the back."

I looked to where he was pointing and found an X made with blue electrical tape. "This blue mark?"

"That's the one."

I took my place on the mark as he picked up a small black device from the podium and joined me. He then took my hand. "Hold on."

With that, Hastings pushed a button on the small remote and the section of the stage we were standing

Chapter Sixteen

on began to sink. Before I knew it, we were underneath the stage, which closed above us, leaving us in total darkness.

"See? Magic."

"Definitely," I said, a little nervous being in a pitch-black room I didn't know. "And dark."

"Oh, sorry," he said. "I forget others don't know these basement rooms as well as I do."

Hastings flicked another switch and the room lit up. I looked up at that gorgeous face of his, and before I could say anything else, he pulled me in for a kiss and said, "I've been wanting to do this since the day I met you."

CHAPTER SEVENTEEN

That was a surprise! Okay, maybe not a total surprise. My first thought as our lips touched was just how soft his were. And how doggone cute he was. I will admit a big part of me had been wanting to kiss him too. But much like the dream I had my first night at Tina's, the reality of me kissing Hastings and not Roger immediately jolted me awake. Figuratively, of course. I wasn't sleepwalking, although who knows since I hadn't been getting any of the real stuff (sleep, that is) since I'd arrived. Not only did I immediately realize how wrong it felt and that I had to find some way to make things right with Roger, but the puzzle pieces as to what might have happened to Maxine started shifting again in my brain.

"I'm so sorry," I said, pulling back. I wasn't sure how I was going to explain all that to Hastings. The sad look he got on that beautiful, beautiful face broke

Chapter Seventeen

my heart. "I... I am so sorry, Hastings, this was... amazing... but I have to go. Can you let Winston know I've gone back to The Françoise?"

With that, I ran toward the first door I found with an "exit" sign on it. It led to a stairwell up to the stage level and then to another door that let me out onto the streets of New York. There, I was met with the scores of fans lined up to greet the actors. To say their faces displayed extreme disappointment that I wasn't who they expected would be an understatement. I lowered my head and walked quickly past them, through the Times Square scrum, and caught a cab that took me up toward Central Park and over to The Françoise.

It was close to midnight by the time I got back to the hotel. I didn't recognize the night doorman, but he sure recognized me.

"Good evening, Ms. Powers," he said after I pushed my way through the revolving door.

I knew they meant all this familiarity to be hospitable, but it still creeped me out that everyone knew who I was. I took a quick look at his name badge. "Thank you, Keiji. Good evening to you as well."

The rest of the lobby was empty: No one at the concierge desk and just one clerk over at the front desk typing something into the computer. Who knows? She might have been playing solitaire like the girl in the show office. I walked over to the lounge where I found a few people sitting in one corner on the couches. No one I recognized. Perhaps everyone was still out on the town—or had already gone up to their rooms. It had been an exhausting few days, and the conference sessions were scheduled to begin again early the following morning.

Then I noticed a group of people spilling out of the rooftop bar elevator in the far corner of the lounge. I walked over to the bar, where I again found Hipster Julio.

"Were they all up at the rooftop bar?" I asked. "Seems kind of late—and cold—to be up there."

Julio looked over at the group. "Oh, no, the rooftop bar closes at 10, which is why we don't have an attendant there anymore. That elevator also goes down to Lafitte's."

"Lafitte's?"

He laughed and rolled his eyes. "Yes, named after the pirate. I think that's what they're calling it at the moment anyway. It keeps changing. Either way, it's a private club within the hotel and available only to members or special groups."

"Kinda like a speakeasy?" I said, thinking of the speakeasy I recently covered at the Lake Tahoe Mountain Lodge.

"Similar. I mean, everyone loves to call their bar a speakeasy these days. It's a thing. But New Yorkers have always loved their private bars and clubs." Julio leaned in conspiratorially. "The story we've been told is that when the first owner built The Françoise, it was the height of Prohibition, so it included a private bar in the basement that connected to his mansion next door. When the home was sold off, the family moved into the penthouse apartment and kept the private room in the basement—and their own private elevator, of course."

Chapter Seventeen

"Of course," I said. I mean, I guess it made sense, right?

Julio smiled and nodded. "After the hotel changed hands, the last remaining family members moved out." He leaned even closer. "Between us, they are not missed."

I laughed. "I can imagine."

"As part of the renovation, Hotels du Jour turned the apartment into the Penthouse Suite and its garden terrace into the rooftop bar. They also redesigned the private bar in the basement. It's not big but very private, and as you may have heard…"

"Discretion is your middle name," I offered.

"Exactly," Julio said, laughing. "Something I'm not always known for, as you may have guessed."

"What? You, Julio? You are the height of discretion."

Julio held out his hands in a mock surrender. "I try! It's not always easy." He laughed. "Anyway, tonight, Mr. Keller and Ms. Berkley hosted a dinner down there for some of the high-end meeting planners here for the conference. They're planning to offer it for private events."

"Very cool," I said. "They didn't show it to us on the tour."

"I think they're only showing it to a select few at the moment," Julio said. "Privacy is part of the cachet. People love getting to do something no one else gets to do."

That exclusivity Georg talked about on his panel, I thought, before seeing Candace exit the elevator with what looked to be the last of the group.

"Thank you, Julio," I said, before walking over to meet her. "Hey, Candace."

"Sam! How are you?" Candace said, giving me a hug and sounding as tipsy as she had the night before.

"Good, you?"

She groaned. "I'm going to need a good month to recover from this conference."

"A lot of wining and dining, eh?"

"Too much, but oh my god, the wines were sooooo good." She laughed before whispering, "Georg even cracked into some of the really good stuff."

"Sassy," I said, offering an eyebrow raise. "Julio was just telling me about the private venue downstairs. Is that something you'd like me to mention in the story?"

Candace's eyes widened. "Oh, yes, please! It's one of those things we offer that's a secret but not a secret, if you know what I mean. It's still a work-in-progress, and we haven't officially unveiled it yet, but we would love to book more private dinners."

"Would you mind showing it to me?"

"Sure," Candace said, gesturing toward the elevator.

"Oh, now?"

"Well, we're here..." Candace shrugged. "I won't be available tomorrow anyway."

"Why not?"

"I have to fly to Prague in the morning to take care of a group at our hotel there."

"Prague! How continental." First Roger, now Candace. Was everyone flying out in the morning?

"*Tres*, or whatever the hell 'very' is in Czech."

Chapter Seventeen

I laughed as Candace and I headed over to the elevator. Hey, I was getting used to not getting any sleep. Might as well take a midnight hotel tour, right? As Julio had indicated, the elevator only had two floors listed: Basement and Penthouse. Candace flashed her key card at the panel and then pushed the button for the basement.

"You need a key card to get the elevator to move?" I asked.

"With this elevator, yes. They want to be able to lock off the elevator in the hours when there isn't a staff person here to oversee entry."

"Does any key card work? Like does mine?"

"No, just employee key cards. Actually, only management-level key cards."

"Interesting."

"These areas used to be private. As we open them up, we're trying to control the access," said Candace. "It's all still a little new for us."

The elevator door opened onto a very well-appointed room. *So this was ole Wentworth's party place,* I thought. In addition to a dining room table set for about a dozen people and a fully stocked bar surrounded by couches and overstuffed chairs in the corner, dark wood-paneled walls held bottles of wine and assorted liquor varieties.

"Does this also serve as the hotel's wine cellar?"

"Kind of. It's for the pricier stuff that our higher-end customers might request in the lounge. Club members will also be able to keep specialty spirits here in these cabinets," Candace said. She pointed to a row of fancy-looking bottles of alcohol in cubbyholes with names etched into the wood next to the bar.

I was surprised to see the table had been cleaned and set. "I thought you said you had a dinner in here?"

"We did, and it was amazing. Too amazing," Candace said, holding her stomach. "The banquet crew came in and cleaned it all up very quickly. That makes me happy since I'm responsible for locking up after them. The employee area is right outside that door so they didn't have far to go." She pointed to a door at the far end of the room. It took me a while to get my bearings, but I realized it was the door I'd seen labeled "private" while exploring the basement level earlier in the day.

As I started looking around the room, I heard a click, and the door she was pointing to opened. Georg entered, looking at us in surprise. I have to admit I was just as surprised to see him.

"Oh, hello, Candace. Ms. Powers."

Again with the formality. Although, since it was the first time I'd seen him since learning he was Hastings' biological father, it felt appropriate.

"Please, again, call me Sam," I said while wondering what he was doing back in the room. Did he forget something? I couldn't see what it might be. The place was pristine.

"Of course." He nodded, smiling but offering no explanation.

"Candace was just showing me this wonderful room for the story I'm writing for *Carmel Today* since she won't be here tomorrow," I continued while checking out the similarities between Hastings and

✦ Chapter Seventeen ✦

Georg, now that I knew they were related. Tall, blue eyes, seductive smile. All there. Still, Hastings had a warmth and unpretentiousness that Georg lacked.

I was cool. "It's so cool." See? Cool.

"Thank you. We came up with the idea when we toured the hotel with our designers after the sale," he said as Candace stifled a yawn. He turned to her. "Candace, why don't you head out? I can show Sam the rest of this venue's offerings."

"Are you sure?" Candace asked.

"Of course. It won't take long, and you have an early day tomorrow."

"So do you."

"Yes, but I'm staying here and don't need to go home to pack."

"That's true. Thank you, Georg. I will see you in the lobby at 7 a.m." Candace turned to me. "Sam, feel free to follow up with any questions you have after you get back home."

"Will do," I said. "Thank you for everything."

Candace gave me a quick hug before leaving through the door Georg had entered.

"I see Candace told you that we are leaving for Europe on the corporate jet in a few hours," said Georg, turning back to me. "We have a group that needs special handling at our hotel in Prague. Candace's assistant will be here to ensure the last day of the conference goes well."

"Yes, she mentioned that when I ran into her upstairs. That's why she was showing me the room now," I said, suddenly a tad uneasy being alone with the man, even if he had never been anything other than utterly charming with me and…

Wait, there's a corporate jet?

"Anyway, as I was saying," he said, "we have similar private clubs and dining options at our hotels in Europe and are excited to introduce the concept here in New York."

"I imagine it will be very popular," I said, looking around at the elegant decor, which included a well-stocked bookcase next to one of the couches. "It's so beautiful. How do people join the club?"

"By invitation only. It's not officially open yet, but we have a few inaugural members and wanted to give some of our top clients a chance to check it out during the conference."

I perused the cubbyholes with names on them behind the bar. I found one for Maxine Martinique with a bottle of Bonheur vodka in it—hard to miss that emerald green bottle. That stopped me in my tracks as more puzzle pieces started falling into place. I realized what was bothering me: The vodka placed next to the bathtub where Maxine died was Laporte, not her preferred brand of Bonheur. That meant it was undeniably staged. Not only that, but this room had a private elevator that allowed entry to the rooftop bar— and thus the Penthouse Suite—without being seen.

As the thoughts continued spinning around in my head, I tried to buy some time by faking a sneeze. I gave myself a good one. You know, the kind that required a tissue.

"Gesundheit," Georg said.

Chapter Seventeen

"Thank you," I responded, fumbling around in my purse pretending to look for a tissue. I found my phone and pushed what I hoped was the voice memo button. I figured it didn't hurt to record our conversation in case I learned something that might be useful later.

I pulled a pack of tissues out. "I sure hope all these late nights and martinis aren't giving me a cold!" I laughed, giving my nose a honk for good measure.

"I'll have some of our famous chicken soup sent up to your room," Georg said, smiling. "It's legendary as a healer."

"Room service runs this late?"

"Twenty-four hours."

"Wow. You really do run a full-service hotel, Georg."

"Always..." he said with pride.

"Sad about Maxine," I said, pointing to the cubby with her name on it.

"Very."

"I hear you had a bit of a history with her," I probed, hoping the phone was recording.

"A long time ago. A lifetime ago, really," he said, sighing.

"And yet, not really a lifetime ago, right?"

"I'm not sure what you mean by that."

I felt the tension rise so deflected. "Well, you're hosting her conference and made Maxine a member of the club."

He visibly relaxed (thank god) and nodded. "She was a valuable client."

Dammit. He had an answer for everything. Maybe I was wrong.

"And Mona?"

Georg responded with a deep sigh. "A great love I lost because of my own stupidity."

Wow. I did not expect that.

"But, as I said, that was all a lifetime ago," Georg said, before switching gears. "I have something I'd like to show you, Sam. An amusing anecdote for your story. Then I'll let you go and have that soup sent up. I'm sure you're exhausted."

"I really am."

Georg pointed me toward the bookcase next to the couch. "It's worth it, I promise."

"Okay…"

"A unique aspect to this room is the secret door the original owner put in."

"Secret door?"

Georg gave the right side of the bookcase a shove, which activated a spring action that caused it to swing open like a door.

"What the…" I said, peering behind the bookcase to find a small hallway.

"It leads to the building next door."

"Into the former owner's mansion?"

"Yes, that's right." Georg got a smile on his face. "Reginald Wentworth built this room to host his gambling parties. Naturally, he wanted access from the basement of his mansion next door."

"Who wouldn't?" I said, laughing. "But I heard he had to sell that building."

"Also correct. Someone did her homework."

"I am writing a story, after all," I said.

✦ Chapter Seventeen ✦

"Wentworth had to sell the building, yes, but he sold it to a consortium of fellow hotel owners," Georg continued. "They used the mansion to create a society for the hospitality professionals of their day with him as one of its members. It was rather ingenious as Wentworth could continue to enjoy both of his creations. The organization grew, ultimately becoming an international association with the original mansion available for members staying in the city."

Georg pulled the door wider, revealing another door at the end of the hallway. It was quite ornate and had what looked like a pineapple carved into it. I recalled seeing one like it on the front door of the mansion next door. I stepped inside to take a closer look.

"What's with the pineapple?"

"That's the international symbol for hospitality," Georg said. "Perfect for the association, of which I happen to be a member. As was my father and his father."

Wait. Access to a private mansion meant Georg could have been in the city—and had access to the hotel—without anyone seeing him. Is that where Maxine went that day she disappeared? As I peered at the door, I didn't notice Georg take a few steps back.

"Unfortunately, that entrance is locked and quite hidden on the other side. As it happens, I'm the only one currently in New York who knows about either entrance."

I spun around. "I'm sorry. What?"

Georg now stood in the doorway. "So sad that you were caught in here without anyone knowing. When

I return in a week or so, we will, of course, try to find you, but I'm guessing it will be too late."

Ah, fuck. I hate when I'm right at the wrong times.

As Georg started closing the door, and with nothing to lose, I asked, "What I don't get is why the rat poison?"

"I don't understand."

"I think you might…"

I looked directly at him and received validation in the form of a smile that was not the smile he used when greeting the staff and guests at the hotel—or when he talked about Mona. Instead, I saw a more malevolent grin that I'm guessing was the reason Tina hated him. "Some things need helping along."

With that, Georg slammed the bookcase door closed. I immediately rushed over and tried pushing it with no success. And that's how I found myself locked in a sealed room only one person knew existed—and that person was a murderer.

CHAPTER EIGHTEEN

Oh, Sam, what have you gotten yourself into? I thought as I took in the absolute silence of the sealed locked room below street level. I looked around the rather industrial-looking hall. It had no windows, but there was a light. No switch, so it probably was on a motion sensor. I'd find out if I stayed still long enough, and it went out. I was so exhausted that a part of me did just want to slump against the wall and take a little nap.

And, okay, maybe I did. It felt so good to sit down, even if it was on the floor. It had been quite the day. A day after a few days of days. I was, quite simply, exhausted. At a certain point, though, just as my eyes grew heaviest and the light did indeed go out, a jolt of adrenaline woke me back up. I wasn't sure if Georg expected me to languish in there for days on end until I died from dehydration, or if he just figured that by the time I did get out, he would already be in an extradition-free country. And that was if anyone believed me that he killed Maxine in the first place. I still had no real proof. Either way, if I didn't start figuring a way out, there was a distinct possibility of that happening.

I waved my arms, and the light came back on. I looked around and thought about my dad's training when I was a kid. He may not have been the warmest of fathers, but as the police chief, he taught me a lot about getting out of sticky situations. The first step was always to take stock of your situation.

Okay, Sam, take stock. Wait, first, let's take off these damn heels.

I took my shoes off. God, that felt good. I stretched my feet out and looked around the room. It was not large. Duh, it was a hallway. Two walls. Two doors. Ceiling. Floor. And no security cameras that I could see or wave at to get someone's attention.

I pulled out my phone and confirmed there was absolutely no cell reception. Nope. Nada. I checked the voice memo app, and it appeared I had managed to record my conversation with Georg. Not that he'd really confessed. "Some things need helping along" wasn't exactly the kind of admission of guilt the police required.

Some things need helping along. Yes, they do, Sam, yes, they do. I turned my attention to the doors. The one on the mansion side with the pineapple looked old. I knew something about old doors. I pushed myself up and walked over to look at it again. The pineapple that was carved into the wood was quite ornate. Was a pineapple really a sign of hospitality?

★ Chapter Eighteen ★

I'd have to take the sociopath's word for it. I tried the handle. Locked. The keyhole looked like it took one of those big old-fashioned type keys. Not the type of lock I could pick—as if I would have been capable of picking a lock anyway. Hey, they make it look easy on TV, right? But, nope, not in my skill set. I knocked. Hard. The door sounded incredibly thick and, according to Georg, was located in a place not many people accessed or maybe even knew existed.

Some things need helping along.

I walked back to the door attached to The Françoise. This one had been updated recently. It had no handle, instead an electronic pad sat on the wall next to it. I'm guessing Georg's key card activated the spring action from this side. I tried my key card. No luck. I then pushed the door. It didn't budge. I felt around the outside. Was there another release for the spring? Nope.

I examined the door more closely. It was then I remembered the book on door repair that Uncle Henry had picked up at the library. Even if there wasn't a handle, there should still be a strike plate and hinge. *Look at me with the lingo!* I found the side of the door with the hinge but didn't see any way to get the pegs out, so I went to the other side where the strike plate should be located. I could see the outer edges where it clicked together with the door jam. Still, it was locked tight. Okay. What about the bottom of the door? To create a pressured swing like it had, there might be some space along the bottom. That made me think of Hastings telling me he used splash blocks to keep the water out of his apartment, which made me think of Tina and the words of wisdom she offered when I first met her.

"Ask for help," she had said. "And make it a party." *Yeah, Tina, but help how? There was no way in hell I could make this a party.*

I felt along the bottom. I wondered if I could find a tool to create more space and then stick something underneath to jiggle the door enough to mimic the pushing action Georg had used to open it. I looked through my bag to see if there was anything that might help and found the sample kit Nadine had given me when they did my makeover. Inside, I found some cosmetics and one of those stainless-steel nail files. I started rubbing it on the bottom of the door to see if I could loosen it or pull it in a way that resembled the bump that caused the door to open. I managed to fit my pinky fingers underneath and tried to jar it back and forth to see if I could get it to click. I started feeling like I might be making progress and gave it a big push when the door flew open. I fell through the space with a force I did not expect and landed on my butt. Luckily, like the carpet in the lobby, it was quite soft. When I looked up, I found Officious Otto standing in front of me.

"We would prefer if you did not damage the property, Ms. Powers," Otto said with a slight smile.

"Oh, Otto, aren't you a sight for sore eyes." Otto offered his hand. I took it and he pulled me up. "How did you know to look for me? It's got to be the middle of the night."

"It is indeed. Almost 2 a.m. I was helping Julio close up the bar when the front desk got a call from a

Chapter Eighteen

certain Maui detective who told us that your phone kept going to voicemail, and there was no answer in your room."

I looked at my phone. "There's no reception in here."

"I believe that is by design."

"How did you find me?"

"Julio told me he last saw you heading down here with Candace."

"Your key card works?"

Otto offered a slight shrug. "I am the head of operations and manager on duty. That requires access to every space in the hotel."

"Did you know about this secret door and hallway?"

Otto peeked behind the bookcase. "I knew something like this might exist. I wasn't quite sure if they'd sealed it up. The previous owners did not allow staff access to this room."

"Georg said it was his little secret."

"He thought a lot of things were secret."

"Like killing Maxine."

Otto bowed his head. "We can't prove anything."

"It isn't a 'discretion is our middle name' kind of thing?"

"It is not."

I took a hard look at him. "Pinky swear?"

Otto stared at me for a long moment before sighing and offering his little finger, which he linked in mine, even though my finger was quite filthy after I'd used it to jiggle the door. "Not when it comes to protecting our people, especially our guests."

"Georg isn't your people?" I asked, pretending not to notice that he wiped his hand with a cloth before putting it back in his pocket.

Otto shook his head. "Not remotely. Those of us who serve The Françoise are family, as are our guests. Outside ownership, not so much."

"Awww. I'm family?"

"Yes, Samantha." I smiled at the use of my first name. "Off the record..." He looked at me, and I nodded. "I can tell you that the previous owners—the descendants of the original proprietor—were not the stewards they should have been. Despite the constraints, we did everything under our power to keep The Françoise operating at the highest standards possible."

I smiled. "You've done a wonderful job."

"We welcomed the capital the new ownership group put into its upkeep. The ol' girl is looking better than she has in a while." He looked around the exquisitely decorated room. "But the core of the hotel has not changed."

"Its people."

He gave a short bow.

"So... what are we going to do about Georg?" I asked. "Do we let him get away with murder?"

"We do not."

But how? I thought. *We don't have a smoking gun, do we?*

I thought of Tina as I asked, "Will you help me?"

Otto bowed again. "I would be honored."

Otto and I started by retracing the steps Georg and Maxine might have taken to get her into the Penthouse

Chapter Eighteen

Suite without anyone seeing. I told him I thought they probably started at the mansion next door. I wasn't yet sure why Maxine met Georg in private but figured that at some point on the day she disappeared, that's where she went. My guess was that they met for a drink at the mansion before Georg offered to show her the secret hallway that led to the private room where we currently stood. Here, he might have plied her with another drink under the guise of inviting her to be in their select club before showing her to the elevator that led up to her Penthouse Suite.

To illustrate my theory, I showed Otto the cubbyhole behind the bar with Maxine's name on it. To my surprise, I discovered it was now empty.

"Oh my god, that's what he was doing here!" I said.

"Excuse me?"

"Candace brought me down to show me the room for my story. Georg interrupted us. I couldn't figure out why he came back."

"And?"

I pointed to the cubbyhole with Maxine's name on it. "There was a bottle of Bonheur vodka in there when I came in earlier."

"Ms. Martinique's favorite."

"See, even you know that! I think that was the bottle spiked with the rat poison."

Otto thought for a moment. "He might have left the bottle in her compartment assuming her death would be ruled accidental. Once Georg was staying here in the hotel, it would be difficult for him to dispose of that bottle without any of the employees seeing him. On top of that, we have security cameras everywhere but in here."

"Can I see where those cameras are placed?"

Otto nodded. We exited through the door and then walked into the staff area. He took me to the room I'd seen earlier with the computer screens. As we entered the room, my cell service was obviously restored as my phone came to life. All of Roger's messages lit up. *Oh wow, I missed a lot.*

"Do you mind?" I asked Otto, who again nodded as he started turning on the monitors.

Since it was still the middle of the night—and I had Otto standing right next to me—I decided to text instead of call. (Feel free to add that to my series of mistakes with the man.)

"Hey there. I'm okay," I wrote. "But thank you for checking on me. Really."

I added a blowing-kiss emoji and a heart to let him know I was serious. I saw a "delivered" and then "read" notification. After a few moments of watching the three dots that meant he was writing something, all I got was a thumbs-up. My heart dropped.

"Still heading home in a few hours?" I wrote.

"Yes."

"Sorry to wake you. Talk soon?"

"Okay."

"Safe travels."

Another thumbs-up. Man, I really screwed the pooch on this one, but I didn't have long to ponder as the security feeds began to appear. I saw images of the lobby, lounge, meeting rooms, hallways on each floor, and the rooftop lounge. I noticed that the camera on

* Chapter Eighteen *

the rooftop lounge angled out toward the bar, leaving the area closest to the elevator unseen.

"That's how he got Maxine into the Penthouse Suite without being seen," I said, pointing to the angle. "But if Georg used his keycard, wouldn't it have been recorded?"

"They could also have used Maxine's key card," Otto said. "I'm going to be honest that we are still getting accustomed to a lot of the technology that Hotels du Jour installed. Much of the information is siloed. For instance, the front desk only has access to guest room data."

"That's why they said the front door to the Penthouse Suite wasn't breached."

"Exactly, because that door hadn't been breached. Georg and Maxine accessed the unit via the back gate and patio doors."

I looked back at the monitors. "Do you have a view of the basement hallway from earlier tonight?"

"Yes," Otto said. We both took seats behind the desk as he pulled up the current feed and then pushed reverse. We sat and watched the empty hallway for a while. Finally, just as my eyelids started to droop, we saw what we needed: Georg walking out of the private room carrying the bottle of Bonheur vodka.

"Bingo."

A few hours later, Otto and I stood discreetly off to the side of The Françoise lobby. Yes, I had a chance to change into comfortable clothes, but no I still hadn't gotten any sleep. Once we saw the security tape, we contacted Detectives Garcia and Anastos. While they were not particularly happy being woken up in the middle of the night, they agreed they had enough to at least hold Georg on the charge of false imprisonment for throwing me into a locked room while they continued their investigation into Maxine's death.

At 7 a.m. sharp, Georg exited the elevator and strode into the lobby with his shiny suitcase thinking he was going to meet Candace. Instead, he was greeted by the two detectives. As they nodded over in our direction, Georg followed their gaze and offered a rueful nod, which I returned. Otherwise, he stood stoically and said nothing as the detectives placed him in handcuffs, took possession of the suitcase containing the laced bottle of Bonheur vodka, and marched him out through a front door—all under the watchful gaze of the portrait of Reginald Wentworth.

CHAPTER NINETEEN

The following night at Tina's, I laid it all out for the assembled crowd. As I had surmised, Georg had not, in fact, "just flown in from Gstaad." He arrived in town early to meet with Maxine in secret at her request. Perhaps not surprisingly, Maxine's wild days—an out-of-control ketamine habit in addition to the vodka—were starting to catch up to her, and she was deeply in debt. Not only in debt but dipping into the Business of Luxury accounts to fund her lifestyle. And Scarlet was starting to catch on.

Maxine learned about Georg's association with Hotels du Jour during the final contract negotiations with The Françoise. She heard he wanted the CEO position, and that Desiree's rather parochial family had been looking for a reason to keep locking him out. Maxine contacted Georg and threatened to tell Desiree about Hastings unless he started helping her out monetarily. Georg agreed and suggested they meet before the conference to discuss the parameters.

On the evening following the final site visit and a visit to her ketamine source, Maxine met Georg at the hospitality association's mansion next door to The Françoise. There, he plied her with drinks before walking her back via the underground tunnel between the two buildings. He showed her the private club and asked if she'd like to be an inaugural member. They commemorated the occasion with a martini made from her favorite vodka, Bonheur, which Georg told her would always be available in her exclusive cubbyhole.

After he knew the rooftop bar had closed and Maxine was starting to get drowsy, Georg offered to walk her up to the Penthouse Suite via the private elevator. They entered the suite via the patio doors, and he stayed with Maxine until she passed out. He started a bath for her, placed her in it, and watched (or helped her along) as she submerged beneath the water.

He set the scene of her "accidental death" using a bottle of the house vodka from the bar in the Penthouse Suite and the vial of ketamine he found in her purse. He set the bottle alongside the tub with her glass, not realizing residue from the spiked bottle remained in one of the olives. Georg then pressed the do-not-disturb and slipped back out through the patio doors so he could conveniently "find" the body with Mona and me two days later—making a point of opening the patio doors on our tour so no one knew they were unlocked.

Chapter Nineteen

All this to keep his wife from learning he'd fathered an illegitimate child when they were first dating. It was hard for me to believe Desiree never suspected. Or maybe she did and that's why she never let him have the CEO position. Also hard to believe Hastings didn't know. With Maxine's blonde hair and Georg's handsome features, once you knew they were his biological parents, it was impossible not to see. He did, of course, lack their sociopathic tendencies. *Thank god, he'd grown up with Tina.*

The gathering at Tina's topped off one of the most perfect days in New York ever. Really. For one, I finally got a good night's sleep. Like 20 hours of sleep. After the police took Georg away and I filled everyone at the hotel in on what had just occurred, I told Mona I was skipping the rest of the conference and went up to my room. I called Roger while he waited for his flight at JFK to let him know everything that had happened and thank him again for calling The Françoise to check on me. Things were still awkward, but I tried my best to make things right. Then I turned on every do-not-disturb I could think of, closed the black-out curtains, crawled into bed, and passed out.

When I finally woke up the following morning, it was around 7 a.m. I looked at my phone, disabled the "Do Not Disturb," and found a message from Mona telling me to knock on our adjoining door when I was awake. After putting on the very sumptuous bathrobe the hotel provided, I opened the door on my side and knocked on hers.

"Mona?"

"I'll be right there, Sam, darling," I heard Mona say, followed by the padding of steps and the click of the lock. She took stock of my groggy face, tousled hair, and bathrobe. "Well, well, aren't we a fashion plate."

"Only the best robes at The Françoise," I said.

"Come in and have some coffee."

"I would love some."

"You're going to need it when you hear about the day I have planned for you…"

"For me?"

"For you, my dear. You are writing about New York for the magazine, are you not?" Mona said, with a gleam in her eye that I hadn't seen since I'd arrived in the city.

"I am."

"Then I'd like to show you New York. My New York." Mona smiled, again looking at my outfit. "You should probably wear comfortable shoes."

An hour later, I was showered and dressed in comfy sneakers, slacks, a tank top, and a cardigan. Yes, the clothes were cotton. I was back to looking like a Californian. Sorry, Nadine and the other *Vogue* stylists, cotton rules.

Mona and I walked down the hall to the elevator, where we found lovely Leonora waiting for us.

"Ms. Reynolds… Sam."

I smiled. "Thank you, Leonora." I nodded, touching her arm briefly. "I mean it, thank you for everything."

"It is my pleasure." Leonora smiled as we rode down to the lobby level, and headed out the front door, getting a tip of the hat from Renaldo as we did.

Chapter Nineteen

"Looks like it's going to be a beautiful day," Renaldo said.

And it was. A perfect spring day, sunny with highs in the low 70s and a light breeze. Mona started us at the Metropolitan Museum of Art, where her friends got us into a sneak peek of the costume exhibit that would be opening at the gala later that month. From there, we wandered down through Central Park—passing the section where I'd had my New York rendezvous with Roger (sigh)—to Midtown, where she showed me her old offices at *Vogue*. After hobnobbing with more ridiculously tall, thin, and stylish folks (a.k.a. Mona's people), we passed through the theater district, the flower district, and a few street festivals before making it to the High Line. We strolled the former railroad tracks now filled with blooming flowers, striking architecture, and imaginative sculptures to the Whitney Museum. Once there, Mona led me up to the museum's third floor and out onto a balcony that offered a gorgeous view of the city that included the Empire State Building in the distance.

"See that," Mona said, pointing to an area between us and the Empire State Building.

"Kind of."

"My first home in the city."

"After Tina's?"

"Yes, after Tina's. My first real apartment. Of my own. It was a studio apartment on the top floor of a five-story walk-up—no elevator—but it was all mine. I was in the big city. And it was magical. And for a long time, this city was my home."

Mona looked wistful as she turned to me and smiled. "And now being back in Carmel is magical. And home." Mona gave my shoulder a hug. "Thank you, Sam, for being there for me this week."

"Anytime."

With that, we grabbed a cab and headed back up to Tina's brownstone for the final dinner. Everyone was there: Winston, Scarlet, Victor, even Harriet and Dmitri, who was happily chatting with Tina's latest two boarders, Naïve Nicole and Emo Emily.

Feeling we should contribute to the potluck, I had the cab driver swing by Aldo's Pizza to pick up a pie for the gang. When I brought it into the dining area, Tina gasped.

"How did you find out about Aldo? He's the best!"

"I happened upon it during one of my walks. That's how you do things in this city, right?"

The pizza was added to the table, along with the usual mixed variety of foodstuffs. Winston whipped up a batch of martinis, using Bonheur vodka, a whiff of dry vermouth, and three olives. We each dutifully ate one of the olives to form a base before making a toast.

"To Maxine. I hope she's found the happiness she was seeking at last," Tina said with a tear in her eye and giving Harriet a small hug.

"To Maxine," we all said. Yet again, I was sorry I'd never met the woman, although I was happy to have had a part in making sure her killer paid for his crime.

"What's going to happen with the conference?" I asked.

★ Chapter Nineteen ★

"Well, we have news on that front," Harriet said. "In consultation with Scarlet, we are dissolving the Business of Luxury."

Scarlet nodded. "But…"

"But," Harriet continued, "we are starting a new venture that I'm hoping you will all help us with. It involves comingling Maxine's extensive list of contacts with the remarkable array of talent radiating out from Tina's brownstone to highlight the inventiveness and innovation that makes this city so special. We are calling it The New Creatives."

"I love it," Mona said. I did, too.

As I listened to the conversations and looked at the group around the table, I realized they really were a family. A big, boisterous family. As were the folks at The Françoise, if a bit more formal and discreet (let's not forget discreet!). As if to solidify the message, Tina brought out a cake decorated with the words "Welcome to the family," placed it in front of me, and enveloped me in one of her famous Tina hugs.

As things were winding down, Mona and I got up to head back to The Françoise. Just then, Hastings walked into the living area. When he saw me, he turned and headed right back out.

"Give me a minute," I said to Mona before rushing out the door. I caught Hastings walking down the stairs.

"Hey there."

Hastings stopped but wouldn't turn to look at me. "Hey, Sam. I'm really sor…"

"Please, don't apologize," I said. "Can we talk?"

Hastings looked up at me with those puppy dog eyes and nodded. *How have you not been taken?* I wondered. "Come here, sit with me," I said, sitting on the top stair outside the brownstone (like a real New Yorker, right?). He came back up the stairs and sat beside me.

"I'm the one who should apologize," I started. "I'm sorry I didn't tell you I wasn't available."

"I should have asked," he said.

"No. I was flirting. I will admit that. I mean, you're adorable. You know that, right? How in the hell are you not taken?" I asked. "Especially when you are surrounded by ridiculously attractive people all day and night."

"I am surrounded by actors and singers and dancers," he said. "They are attractive, but they are also, how should I say this… artistic…?"

I laughed. "Ah, those pesky artistic types, huh? I'm guessing you've cycled through quite a few of them."

He finally smiled. "I've done okay. Maybe it's been easier, you know, cycling through artistic types, than dealing with my somewhat unconventional family."

"I'm sorry your biological parents were a challenge. But your family, your real family—that group sitting in there as we speak—is pretty darn amazing."

Hastings smiled and looked back at the house. "They kinda are, huh?"

"I'm a little jealous."

Hastings looked at me. "I'm going to guess you have more people on your side than you realize."

"Are you going to tell me I just have to ask for help?"

★ Chapter Nineteen ★

"And make it a party," he said in his best impression of Tina.

We both laughed.

Hastings took my hand. "Friends? Unless, of course, circumstances change in some way…"

Oh yeah, that's just what I need—another paramour who lives 2,000 miles away, I thought. I just smiled and nodded. "Friends."

CHAPTER TWENTY

I flew home the next day, pondering how my New York story might go. Obviously, the focus was the renovation of The Françoise. The restoring to glory of a historic gem in a way that combined the hotel's rich—and often notorious—history with a modern sensibility, and a staff that goes above and beyond in making every guest feel welcome. I would also, of course, call out all the wonderful sights: the Met, Broadway, the High Line, Tribeca art galleries, and the overall hustle and bustle of the city.

Yes, that includes the noise, except, as I learned, below ground. I realized the noise level was symbolic of the city's energy. There's a reason for New York's status as the ultimate center of the action, be it creative or financial or academic or fashion or publishing. Perhaps that's why there were so many songs written

Chapter Twenty

about making it big in the city. All that hustle adds up to, well, a lot.

For this California girl, the city offered the ultimate in adventures, and it did inspire me, but I didn't think I could live there. I appreciated how some thrived on that energy. How could you not, with everything you could ever want found right outside your door? How amazing is that? People like Tina and Victor and Scarlet and Winston fed on that dynamism. Same with the people at The Françoise.

For others, it kind of ate them up. That lust for status and prestige ultimately did in people like Maxine and Georg. And yet, somehow, they produced Hastings. Adorable, adorable Hastings. Luckily, he had Tina and Horatio and their cohorts bringing him up. I hoped he was going to be okay but kind of knew he would be with that group supporting him.

Back in Carmel, I decided to use my energy from the New York trip to tackle our issues with the house. Using Tina's advice—"Ask for help. And make it a party."—I told Uncle Henry that we should schedule a work day/party and ask Dad's friend Al to coordinate our efforts since he had proved to be so handy at the police station. Henry thought it was a great idea.

Henry said that Al had been visiting my dad almost every afternoon, so on my first day back, I headed over to the assisted living facility. I walked out to the courtyard and found Al and my dad in almost exactly the same positions I'd left them before

I went to New York. I regaled them with my tales of the city before asking Al if he would like to help us out. Before I could even get the words out, he said, "I accept."

Al came and toured the house while Henry and I pointed out the various problems. He gave us a list of tools to have on hand, which Henry said he would take care of as I gathered the troops. That Friday afternoon, Lizzy, a couple of Lizzy's brothers, our friends Jen and Holly, plus Mona and some of the staff from *Carmel Today*—including, I was surprised to see, FU Chelsea, even if she was somewhat useless—arrived at the house. I made sure we had plenty of drinks (no martinis!) and food on hand and put on some tunes. Al strode around barking instructions, looking happier than I'd seen him. Since he was making my dad so happy, I was glad I could make him happy. I was also pleased that the house was getting some love, not to mention knowing Al was available the next time something fell apart.

At one point, when I headed into the kitchen to grab a soda, Mona joined me.

"I hear you talked to Scarlet," she said.

"I did! She was nice enough to look at our finances and offered to create a household fund to cover Dad, Henry, and me."

"I'm glad," Mona said, looking over at Henry, doing his best to file the edges of the door around the strike plate under Al's critical eye. That kind of labor was definitely not in Henry's wheelhouse, but somehow the fact he was trying made him look even more charming. Mona smiled and then turned to look

Chapter Twenty

at me. "Sam, I've been trying to figure out how to say thank you for all you did for me in New York."

"There's no need for that," I said. "Heck, you got me the job at the magazine, and you helped get some of these people here. That's plenty."

"It's really not. I was thinking that after our editorial meeting on Monday, it might be a good idea for you to take a vacation."

"Vacation?"

"Lizzy told me it might be a good idea for you to visit Hawaii," Mona said.

Hawaii, eh?

Mona handed me an envelope. Inside, I found a voucher for a round-trip ticket to Hawaii.

"Really?"

"Really."

I gave Mona a hug, and she went to join Uncle Henry. I saw her give him a kiss on the cheek, which he returned with a smile. They clasped hands, and it warmed my heart. After all she'd been through, it made me happy to know she was loved by a man as good as Henry.

I took a deep breath and walked outside to the succulent garden my mom had planted. You know, to pull some weeds. Once there, I sat on the bench, pulled out my phone, and called Roger. Thank god, he picked up.

"Hello, Sam."

"Aloha, Roger. How's it going?"

"Fine. What do you want?"

Ouch. Still icy. But I was going to push through even if it killed me. "Well, you will be happy to hear things are much better here. I'm hosting a house-fix-up party. And get this, Scarlet looked at our finances and is helping…"

"I'm glad to hear that. Listen, I kind of have to run…"

"Please, please don't go without hearing me out."

He paused for a moment before saying, "Okay."

"I'm sorry."

"Sam, you've already apologized."

"Not just for New York. I'm sorry for expecting you to be there for me all the time and not doing the same. I'm sorry for not believing in us…" I started to tear up and fought it as best I could. "I mean, you know, these last few years have been a lot."

His voice got softer. "I know."

"But it's no excuse for sabotaging the best thing that's happened to me in a long time."

"Best thing, huh?" I could hear a grin in his voice. (It's possible to hear a grin through a phone, you know.)

"By far the best thing…"

"You weren't wrong that we have a lot going against us," he said. "Starting with the distance. And I know I was a little cranky in New York."

"A little cranky?"

Thank god, he laughed. "Just a smidge."

"So… what if I were to help alleviate the distance thing?"

"You got a row boat?"

I laughed. "You going to meet me halfway in your kayak?"

"Always." And there it was, the voice that made me go weak in the knees.

Chapter Twenty

"Like you did in Central Park?"

"Yes, even in that godforsaken city."

He really didn't like New York. I wouldn't hold that against him, as much as I had come to love the place myself.

"How about if I told you that you wouldn't have to meet me halfway?"

"I'm listening…"

"Well, as a thank you for my help, Mona offered me a round-trip ticket to Hawaii," I said. "Any island I'd like. I don't suppose you have any suggestions."

"Maui is nice this time of year."

"Oh, yeah, what part of Maui?"

"I know a nice little bungalow between Paia and Makawao that might have space for you."

"Oh? How about the amenities? As you know, I'm used to the best."

"It's no Françoise, but it has its own charms."

"But is discretion your middle name?"

"Absolutely! When might you be visiting?"

"Is tomorrow too soon?"

"Tomorrow would be perfect."

"I was hoping you'd say that, although okay, it might be next Tuesday."

Roger laughed. Oh, how I liked that laugh.

"That works, too. I have some comp days coming to me, so I will ask for some time off."

"Okay, then, we're set."

"Can't wait."

With that, and perhaps fueled by the energy of the city I'd just left, I went back inside with a skip in my step. And the following Tuesday, I caught my flight to Maui. It would be my first time back to Hawaii since my initial press trip for *Carmel Today* magazine, the journey that launched me into the world of travel writing and led me to Roger.

I realized how much I'd grown since that trip. The pains of the past—my mom's death, my manipulative ex-boyfriend, my dad's diagnosis—were finally starting to fade. Instead, positive images like those of the group of people helping me with the house and the crew back in New York started to take over. With newly acquired strength and something that felt a lot like hope in tow, I headed back to Maui.

THE END

Book Club Questions

1. When travel writer Samantha Powers arrives in New York City, the first thing she notices is the noise level. What's the first thing that comes to mind when you think of the city?

2. Describe some of the personal challenges Sam is dealing with in this book. Can you relate to the decisions she makes? What is the most important lesson she learns?

3. Is The Françoise Hotel somewhere you would like to visit? Why? What about the other sights Sam visits?

4. What insights does Sam gain from the various people she meets on the trip? How do they relate to her current life?

5. What did you think when the body was found? Could it have been accidental?

6. Did you guess the person responsible or the reason why? Which clues gave that person away?

7. Which of Mona's friends in New York or staff members at The Françoise was your favorite? Do you know people similar to any of the characters in the book?

8. How do you feel about Sam's ongoing romance with Roger, the Maui detective she met in the first book? Do you think they have a future together? What about Hastings? Do you think she will see him again?

9. Sam samples a number of martini styles during her time in New York. Do you have a preference for how one is made?

10. Where do you think Sam will travel to next?

About the Author

In her 20+ years as a writer and editor, Ann Shepphird has covered everything from travel and sports to gardening and food to design and transportation for a variety of publications.

Now Ann is tackling her favorite topics—mysteries and rom-coms—for 4 Horsemen Publications. The Destination Murder Mysteries combine Ann's experiences as a travel journalist with her stint working for a private investigator while the University Chronicles series of rom-coms are based on her days as a college-level communications instructor.

Ann lives in Santa Monica, California with her longtime partner Jeff and their furry companions Melody and Winnie. When she's not writing, Ann is most likely to be found on a tennis court or in her garden.

Discover more at
4HorsemenPublications.com

10% off using HORSEMEN10

www.ingramcontent.com/pod-product-compliance
Lightning Source LLC
LaVergne TN
LVHW041800060526
838201LV00046B/1061